"Can't you guess why I had to come?"
Matt murmured into her hair.

"You know that the more time we spend together," Nita said, "the more I'll care about you—and the more I'll be hurt."

He fingered the lace edging on her robe. "I just couldn't stay away," he said at last. "I came for the same reason I want to lose when we argue and I take you in my arms, even though I know each time I do will make it harder to let you go. I can't help myself. When you smile I lose track of everything except the color of your eyes and the way your face lights up. I couldn't begin to explain why it takes my breath away, but it does."

"Then forget just for now that we don't have a future," she whispered. "Love me, Matt. . . ."

WHAT ARE *LOVESWEPT* ROMANCES?

They are stories of true romance and touching emotion. We believe
those two very important ingredients are constants in our highly sensual
and very believable stories in the *LOVESWEPT* line. Our goal is to give
you, the reader, stories of consistently high quality that may sometimes
make you laugh, sometimes make you cry, but are always fresh and
creative and contain many delightful surprises within their pages.

Most romance fans read an enormous number of books. Those they
truly love, they keep. Others may be traded with friends and soon
forgotten. We hope that each *LOVESWEPT* romance will be a
treasure—a ''keeper.'' We will always try to publish

LOVE STORIES YOU'LL NEVER FORGET
BY AUTHORS YOU'LL ALWAYS REMEMBER

The Editors

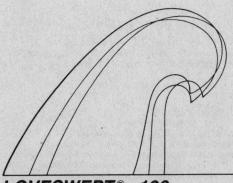

LOVESWEPT® • 196

Hertha Schulze
Solid Gold Prospect

BANTAM BOOKS
TORONTO • NEW YORK • LONDON • SYDNEY • AUCKLAND

SOLID GOLD PROSPECT

A Bantam Book / June 1987

LOVESWEPT® and the wave device are registered trademarks of Bantam Books, Inc. Registered in U.S. Patent and Trademark Office and elsewhere.

If you would be interested in receiving protective vinyl covers for your Loveswept books, please write to this address for information:

Loveswept
Bantam Books
P.O. Box 985
Hicksville, NY 11802

ISBN 0-553-21771-2

Published simultaneously in the United States and Canada

Bantam Books are published by Bantam Books, Inc. Its trademark, consisting of the words "Bantam Books" and the portrayal of a rooster, is Registered in U.S. Patent and Trademark Office and in other countries. Marca Registrada. Bantam Books, Inc., 666 Fifth Avenue, New York, New York 10103.

PRINTED IN THE UNITED STATES OF AMERICA

O   0 9 8 7 6 5 4 3 2 1

One

Nita Holiday clapped the black fedora on the back of her head with one hand, gritted her teeth, and cocked her right leg into a giant step in the air. The photographer had chosen this pose as the essence of carefree abandon. How could he be so wrong? But the concussion she'd get if she fell over backward was the least of her worries. The temperature had to be over a hundred under the studio lights. Sweat, drawn up through her makeup by heat and exertion, beaded her forehead beneath her hat brim, and an oversized shocking-pink sweater and skintight black leather pants compounded her discomfort. Modeling didn't get its reputation as a glamour job from anyone who'd done any.

"More right angle on that leg, Nita," the photographer called. "Keep it spontaneous."

He bent over the camera's viewfinder, reflections gleaming off his bald head like rays of inspiration. Would he demand more extravagant contortions? Nita wondered. *Were* there any? For the moment he seemed satisfied and beckoned the two leggy teens who were doubling with her in the shot.

"All right then, darlings. Let's add your leaps. Knees high. Think colts loose in spring pastures. Toss those heads."

They bounded forward, their buoyancy seemingly undiminished by wearing heavy clothing at jungle temperatures. Their energy amazed Nita. Adolescent metabolism? she mused. Youthful high spirits? The endless cans of soda they consumed? A searing cramp cut short her theorizing.

"Damn!" she yelped, clutching her calf.

The photographer looked martyred. "Sensational leaps, darlings, but we lost our right angle."

"Sorry," Nita groaned, massaging her leg.

His assistants converged in a hasty consultation. When time was money, tempers frayed easily. "Rotten luck," one of them said. "The leaps were *fabulous*."

"Putting a block under her foot will ruin the line."

"She could be tying her shoe or something."

"How *banal!*"

Several pairs of eyes rolled ceilingward in unison, but any pose that didn't defy the laws of gravity sounded great to Nita. Wit wasn't a quality she normally required from her knee joints, and her leg had strong reservations about more originality.

One of the assistants broke out of the huddle to fetch a two-foot block covered in the same gleaming white paper used as background for the shot. "Now we'll have to retouch when we print," he complained as he set it down beside her.

She grinned in spite of her pain. "About time you guys did a little honest work."

"Let's go, darlings," the photographer called.

Propping her black leather sneaker on the block, Nita held out the laces to display her yellow-tipped nails against the chartreuse socks.

They were sensational.

When the shooting ended, the two girls sprinted for the dressing room like children let out of school. Nita plucked off her hat to shake loose her wheat-blond hair and followed at a more sedate pace. On her way out she planted a light kiss on top of the photographer's gleaming pate. "Terrific session."

"Incredible girls, aren't they? Like two dewy roses."

With a good-natured grimace, she shrugged off the way he'd excluded her in his remark. "Bloom's the word these days."

After stepping out of her outfit in the dressing room, Nita automatically checked her slim figure in the mirrored walls. She might not be dewy, she thought, but there was nothing wrong with her stem. Maybe admirers of a certain kind of bloom might be in for a disappointment near the top.

The girls, whose bodies throbbed faintly to music from the radio perched on the counter, chattered about their next assignment while they peeled off false eyelashes. It was only April, but they were off to Paris to shoot a spread for the October issue of *Vogue*. It would confirm their status as two of the Harrison Agency's hottest new models. A wave of nostalgia reminded Nita of the European assignment that had launched her own career at Harrison five years ago.

The blond girl leaped to her feet. "Take my chair, Nita."

"What's this?" she asked with a lift of one eyebrow. "Pity for the aging and decrepit?"

Still, she was glad to sit down. She pulled back her hair and slathered cream onto her face with strokes that moved upward and outward from long habit. The girls did the same, dissolving gradually from sirens into freckle-faced kids with shaggy brows and mouths like swollen fruit. Her own face didn't change as much.

With a tissue in her hand, she peered into the mirror. The contrast between her image and the girls' gave her something to think about in a business built on youth and changing styles. Should she have agreed to crop her hair to match the blonde's masculine cut? Her refusal had caused an uproar at the agency because Harrison models were forbidden to cross their photographers. At the time, she had said no because she'd asked herself what man would want a head of hair like his own in bed with him? Not, unfortunately, that she had anyone special in mind.

The brunette, pausing in a rehearsal of her repertoire of pouting expressions, checked her watch and let out a shriek of dismay. "I have to run! My mom's meeting the four-thirty commuter train. Come on, if you're coming."

In her haste to follow, the blonde grabbed for the radio and knocked Nita's shoulder bag off the counter.

An arsenal of creams, mascaras, lip rouges, hair spray, combs and brushes, bottles of perfume and nail polish rattled across the floor, accompanied by the slither of packets of tissues, a half-dozen of the romantic novels she devoured during the long waits while her hair was being styled, a sheaf of checkbooks, and the mail she'd been too rushed to read that morning.

"Oh, Lord! I'm sorry."

"Don't worry." Nita smiled at the stricken face. "I'll get it. You catch your train."

Left alone in the dressing room, she crouched to gather her belongings. Among the bills and junk mail an envelope bearing the Harrison logo caught her eye. Surprised, she slit it open with one yellow nail. Her expression froze as she read:

Dear Benita,

As you know, at Harrison we make every effort to work with each girl on her plans for the future. After reviewing the decline in requests for you over the past six months, we feel it's time for you to move on to a new phase in your career.

Freshness is vital to the Harrison image and we believe you, too, would prefer to be remembered at your peak. Naturally, we want this transition to be as happy as the rest of your association with us, so let us know if we can help in any way.

All the best,
Arlene Harrison

Nita stared at the letter. Models had short careers; she'd been realistic about that from the beginning. But she'd planned to retire on her own terms, and not until she'd built a nest egg to start a business of her own. Numbers and half-formed plans skittered through her mind. Without her modeling fees she'd have to rethink her lifestyle as well as her career.

"At least I kept my hair," she muttered under her breath.

She quickly tossed on her clothes and glimpsed her face in the mirror as it emerged from the neck of her sweater. Bloom free; practically haggard. No wonder the focus of the camera had been on her knees all afternoon. She untied her hair to let the pale strands fall free for a moment. Did it help? She wasn't sure. Seldom dismayed, she took this sudden sense of vulnerability as a bad sign. If her brains went the way of her looks, she'd be in big trouble.

She sleeked back her hair with a floppy bow at the nape of her neck, then shrugged into her fox jacket and slung her heavy bag over one shoulder. "If you mope," she scolded her reflection, "you shouldn't mope alone."

So on her way out, she stopped at the telephone and dialed her best friend's office number. Liberty Faulkner interrupted before she'd said two sentences. "What's wrong?" Libby asked.

"It's that obvious, huh?"

"To me it is."

"Why try to hide my shame?" Nita proclaimed in theatrical tones. "I'm a has-been. Kaput. Over the hill. Out on my elegant derrière."

"What are you babbling about?"

"Harrison is letting me go. Can you believe it? Right before the baseball season. They may have blondes to burn, but where will they find one who can touch me at first base?"

"There must be some mistake."

Nita groaned. "You bet. Mine—when I told Parker Beineke to hire a man if he wanted a model with a crew cut, when I turned down an assignment in Chile for *Redbook* so I could hear Mark solo at Carnegie Hall, when I blew all that money on redecorating the apartment, when—"

Libby cut in firmly. "Sounds as though you should come for dinner tonight. We can talk while Blake cooks. He's invented this incredible new lasagna."

"Food is your answer to every problem."

"Better than drink. Look, I have to stop at the library for a minute on my way home. Meet me in Rare Books."

"With the moldy and worm-eaten? Is that symbolic?"

"You *are* in a mood. I'll see you in fifteen minutes."

• • •

Choosing a seat down the table from the only male in Rare Books that afternoon, Nita had plenty of time to brood over the difference between Libby's situation and her own. Libby was in the second year of a deliriously happy marriage to a photographer who could have walked right out of the pages of one of Nita's romances. And only last winter Libby had been appointed to a full-time position in Columbia University's French Department. Not Nita's idea of a dream job, but she couldn't argue with the palpable aura of contentment that overspread her friend's life. Today she wouldn't sneer at being half as lucky. Either half would do.

A chair scraped at the other end of the table, but she paid no attention. Then the lean, tanned fingers of a masculine hand thrust a fly-spotted sheet of paper into her line of vision and its owner stirred the air by bending over her.

"Excuse me," he said.

Raising her head, she confronted a tanned chest tunneling down to a deep-pocketed navel as the stranger's movement made his partially opened shirt fall away from his body. In Butler Library, a glimpse of smooth skin sleeking over hard muscles had more shock value than a naked man strolling along a public beach. Her color rose—and then rose higher for rising at all.

She shifted her gaze from the stranger's chest to his profile, barely inches away from her face. Three small moles sketched the angle of a determined jaw near an earlobe whose seductive roundel of flesh, framed in a mass of shaggy dark hair, thrust outward slightly. Staring at its downy fragility as though she had never seen that part of a man's anatomy before, she fought back a sudden impulse to test its softness between her teeth. Could losing her job trigger a mental breakdown in an otherwise stable woman? she wondered.

"Can you make anything of this?" he asked.

She swallowed a lump in her throat. "Of what?"

"This letter."

"Me? Are you kidding?"

"Take a good look. I'd really appreciate it."

He snagged a nearby chair, and while he pulled it over to sit beside her, she studied the hatchetlike planes of his cheekbones, his angular nose, dark eyes with a crackle of laughter in their depths, and a firmly drawn mouth whose underlip was even more tempting than the ear. She knew she was staring like a yokel, but she couldn't resist. What was a man like this doing in a *library?*

"I came all the way from Michigan to see it," he continued with a rueful expression, "and I can't decipher a single word."

She blinked and tore her gaze from his face, more to recover her equilibrium than because she expected to be of any help. The writing on the worn page looked as though a chicken had been scratching it for gravel. "This is English?"

"French."

"Oh."

"About 1665."

"Oh?"

Her sidelong glance caught his grin. "Okay," he said, "I confess. Asking you was just an excuse for speaking to the prettiest woman I've seen since I came to town."

"Oh?"

With repartee like this he'd probably class her among the original dumb blondes, she thought. Nevertheless, a warm feeling of satisfaction blossomed in the pit of her stomach. What did the Harrison Agency know? She might have lost her job and her ability to string together two words at a time, but her appeal was intact.

"I've been staring at that page all afternoon," he said. "If you can't help me translate, how about cheering me up over a cup of coffee?"

Stranger in town, she thought. The oldest line in the book, but her instinct didn't hesitate. Savvy had gone the way of coherent speech. She was already reaching for her bag when Libby arrived. For the first time in their long friendship, Nita wasn't delighted to see her.

"All set," Libby whispered, but as she took in the stranger's proprietary grip on the back of Nita's chair, her brows rose in a query. "Did I keep you waiting too long?"

"Lord, no!" Nita said.

A knowing twitch dented the corner of Libby's mouth; Nita waved vaguely at the manuscript page. "He was asking me about this letter. It's in French."

"Really?"

"Take a look," the stranger said quickly. The shift in his attention struck Nita like a personal loss, although he smiled at her as he handed the page to Libby.

Libby plucked her glasses from her curly dark hair, settled them on her nose, and bent to skim the contents. French interested her even more than food. "I didn't realize Columbia had any firsthand material on early Jesuit missionaries," she said. "How did you persuade the archivist to come up with this treasure?"

The man's dark eyes glinted. "Determination—and a fortune in long-distance phone calls. When I turned up in person, she still wanted to check everything from my birth certificate to how well I'd washed my hands before she let me look at it."

Libby laughed. "That sounds like Miss Alcott."

"But you knew what the letter was about," he said. "That means you can read it."

"Given a bit of time, I could."

"Can we talk?"

Hesitating, Libby glanced at Nita. "Why don't we go outside?" Something in Nita's expression made her add, "My husband's coming by to pick me up on his way home."

"Be right with you."

While the man replaced the fragile page with the pile of notes and the backpack at his end of the table, Libby leaned down to whisper, "You look as though that man hit you over the head with a club. Who is he?"

"No idea."

"A total stranger?"

In spite of years of sharing confidences, a wave of unaccustomed warmth flushed Nita's face when Libby's brown eyes widened. Smiling weakly, she said, "Some of my best friends spend time in libraries."

Libby chuckled. "But only you could turn up a sexy man in Rare Books!"

On their way outside, the three met Miss Alcott herself hobbling down the corridor, wearing over her nondescript dress the universal archivist's uniform: a sagging brown sweater. Although the curve of her spine threatened to focus her vision permanently at a spot on the floor just ahead of her toes, she managed an affable nod at the stranger.

"Find what you wanted, Mr. Lamartine?" she asked.

He grinned down at her. "I'm getting warm."

"Good. Let me know how your project turns out."

"Will do. You've been a terrific help."

As his bronzed hand enfolded the one Miss Alcott offered him, Libby poked Nita. "Look at that," she whispered in an awed voice. "She acts almost as impressed as you."

"Lamartine," Nita murmured.

Libby rolled her eyes. "At least *she* checked out his references first!"

Matt Lamartine's profession—as he told Libby and Nita while they waited for Blake at the foot of the library steps—was mining engineering. He'd driven to New York during spring break from his teaching job at the Michigan Technological University in Houghton in order to get one last piece of evidence for a research project about ore fields around eastern Lake Superior. The missionary's letter, written from Canada to his Jesuit superiors, was supposed to recount seventeenth-century finds of gold and amethyst. Matt hoped it would provide a clue to their exact locations.

Nita's abstraction during Matt's explanation drew Libby's pointed looks, but she ignored them. Simply standing beside this man absorbed all her attention. Her body vibrated with awareness of his presence the way the young models had responded to the music in their dressing room. Listening less to his words than to his voice, she breathed in the tender, moist air that was April's belated gift to the city. Without glancing in his direction, she felt his dark gaze warming her face.

"I had sense enough to bone up on my French before I came," he was saying, "but it never occurred to me that the Palmer method wasn't around in 1665. Until you turned up, I thought I'd have to start back empty-handed tonight."

The last word registered. Tonight? Nita's sense of timeless contentment fell away in one stroke. He couldn't be leaving tonight! Definitely not the schedule she'd had in mind. In a matter of hours he might be gone. Retrieving her wits and her voice, she exclaimed, "Libby could transcribe your letter and . . . and I could send it to you."

Libby's mischievous smile forgave this high-handedness, but her husband, arriving just in time to hear Nita giving away a generous chunk of his wife's leisure time, regarded the offer with unconcealed astonishment. "Since when is Old French one of your interests, Nita?"

"Semi-old. 1665."

"Is that supposed to explain something?"

Libby telegraphed her husband a meaningful look. "She's trying to do Mr. Lamartine a favor."

"I think I'm being taken in hand," Matt said.

Blake laughed. "In that case, protest is useless. I know these two. Are you joining us for dinner?"

"What a *marvelous* idea," Libby said quickly, "but we've already promised to have dinner out tonight. In fact, we'll be late if we don't hurry."

"I thought I was—"

Libby stepped lightly on her husband's foot.

He responded as though on cue. "That's right! Wiener schnitzel Friday. How could I forget?"

"Call me tomorrow, Nita," Libby said as Blake put one arm around her shoulders to draw her away. "I'll be happy to work on that letter. You two can arrange everything."

From the amusement in Matt's eyes as he turned to her after Blake and Libby had gone, Nita knew he hadn't missed any of this byplay. She couldn't begin to guess what conclusions he'd drawn. How could she read his mind? Her own was barely functioning.

"Nice folks," he said.

"They're special. If there's gold in that letter, Libby will find it for you."

"Speaking of gold . . ." He thrust his hands deep into the pockets of his jeans and studied the sidewalk. "I was all set to buy you coffee, but my budget isn't geared to elegant city dining. Any chance you're one of those liberated women?"

"Liberated enough to go dutch?"

"I could try to make it up to you in fine talk." His smile made common sense seem even less relevant.

"For that I might cook."

"Then it's a deal." He fell in beside her as they retraced their steps to collect his backpack. The harmony in their movements gave her another unexpected jolt of pleasure. "But I'll be fair. You deserve a sample before you commit yourself to a hot stove. Anyone ever told you your eyes are bluer than a pool reflecting back a summer sky?"

"Not bad," she said, laughing.

"Are you hinting I'll have to do better if you cook as good as you look? How about bluer than a patch of bluebells in the spring?"

"Sounds like you have a whole routine."

"For ordinary occasions, but it seems to have slipped my mind. Something about you beggars my normal powers of description."

She smiled to herself. Corny, but easy going down.

"The truth is"—he paused for a moment—"your eyes are bluer than anything I've ever seen."

His altered tone made her glance up at him, and when she did their gazes locked with an intensity that seemed to shake him as much as it shook her. They stopped halfway up the library steps, oblivious to the students descending in groups of twos and threes.

"Bluer than anything," he repeated softly.

"Yours are brown."

"Well," he said, letting out his breath with a shaky laugh, "now that we've got that settled, I'd better get my stuff before they close up shop in there."

She watched him turn and take the remaining steps

two at a time, not knowing whether he ran out of eagerness to rejoin her or in flight from the same wild elation that was drumming in her heart.

They shopped for groceries at the Gristede's around the corner from her apartment. As if they shared awareness of the explosive potential in physical contact, each avoided brushing shoulders or fingertips with the other as they chose cans from the shelves, felt the produce for firmness, and argued somewhat distractedly over their likes and dislikes.

For convenience, Nita preferred frozen foods. Matt insisted on fresh, swearing she'd never revert to old habits once he showed her how to cook them his way. They compromised on fish instead of the steak Nita wanted or the vegetarian meals he claimed were part of his training regimen for another summer of prospecting in the Ontario wilderness.

"What about these for dessert?" she called to him from a display of kiwi fruit.

"Kind of hairy looking, aren't they?"

"They're supposed to have that fuzz."

"Ah, the wonders of the metropolis. I keep forgetting that you can get anything here."

"Come on. Houghton's not that small."

"Ever been there?"

"My family's from Chicago. The Upper Peninsula was my summer playground as a kid. We had a place on the lake about thirty miles from Houghton. You and I practically grew up neighbors."

"Except I lived on the wrong side of the tracks." The mockery in his voice was light but unmistakable.

"It's gorgeous country around there."

"Sure it is. That's why Chicago people love coming up for a week or two every summer to rough it in their twelve-room cottages and flash hundred-dollar bills at the natives. You probably felt like pioneers because you had to double up on the bathrooms, right?"

His reaction made her regret mentioning the lake house. She'd thought only of the fact that they'd both lived in the same area. Why hadn't she remembered that the gap between summer people, who came for a few lazy weeks on the shore, and the people who called the isolated reaches of northern Michigan home year-round, loomed larger than the bond?

"Something like that," she admitted, adding the kiwi fruit to their basket without looking at him. "But the plumbing went out at least once all the same."

"Not to mention the black flies, poison ivy, sunburn—"

"Don't put words in my mouth," she interrupted with more heat than she intended. "I loved those summers."

"In spite of everything?"

"In spite of being what you call a 'Chicago person'!"

"Somehow I can't picture you more than a block from the heart of the city."

"What are you?" she asked, following him to the checkout line. "A specialist in stereotypes?"

"Some kinds."

"You sound as though you've been on the receiving end."

"I've learned to handle that, but I get tired of hearing small farmers labeled greedy, miners labeled trouble-makers, and Indians labeled drunks."

"So just to even things out you decide everybody from Chicago has to be either a snob or a phony? And I thought college professors were logical."

Despite his steady look, a faint flush appeared under his tan. "We've been known to lapse under stress."

"*All* of you?"

"The ones susceptible to corrupting influences."

"You mean to addictive luxuries like credit cards and indoor plumbing?"

A glint of humor flashed in his eyes, but the wariness remained. "Actually, I was thinking more of liberated women."

He set their basket down in front of the cashier, and while the total mounted on the register, he began to empty his wallet. Nita pushed the bills back into his hand. "Now, look, you don't have to—"

"Groceries I can handle."

"We had a deal."

"I seem to have muffed my end of it."

"Oh, I don't know. The liberated women line was kind of sweet. And if I burn the dinner, we'll be even again."

"Think that would do it?" He hoisted the bag as though it were filled with feathers. "If you won't let me pay, I won't make you carry."

They walked to her apartment in silence, his thoughts a mystery, hers too filled with contradictions to make conversation possible. The man was an unknown quantity, almost a stranger. Clearly part of his breadth of shoulder came from the chip he carried there, yet his sensitivity about the place where he grew up was as difficult to comprehend as the reason why she'd accepted his initial invitation without a second thought. Was she simply reacting to Mrs. Harrison's letter? A need to prove she was still attractive might not be a noble motive, but it wasn't as crazy as being bowled over by a sexy earlobe.

After she unlocked her door, Matt stepped into her living room gingerly, as though it had been mined for his arrival. He whistled at what he saw. "You have a place like this all to yourself?"

"Before she got married, Libby and I used to share."

"Looks like you tore it right out of a magazine."

"I had it redone last month."

"Was that less bother than spring cleaning?"

His mild sarcasm gave her a fresh reason to regret her extravagance. If he wrote her off as simply something out of a country club and the society pages, their relationship might set some kind of record: peaking and going on the skids within a single hour.

She retrieved the bag of groceries. Pausing on her way to the kitchen to watch him cross the pastel room, she saw it suddenly through his eyes. If he expected to find a reflection of her own tastes, he'd be disappointed. Kazjanian and Co. had chosen the peach fuzz and glitter look; she'd only paid the bills.

With his pack slung over one shoulder, he made no

sound as he moved across the thick pale carpet. He
seemed more rough-hewn in this environment than he
had in the book-lined library and reminded her of a
stag stalking through a foreign forest, taking possession of its textures and smells. He turned over one of
the peach velour pillows, ran a finger along the edge of
a chrome-and-glass étagère filled with color-coordinated
bibelots, and picked up a couple of romances from the
coffee table. He skimmed a page or two, frowning with
puzzlement.

"I give up," he said, facing her with the books in his
hand. "Except for these, this room might as well still
be in the store. What do you do here?"

"Not a whole lot. I'm out most of the time."

"Idling with the idle rich?"

"Will you cut that out!"

He glanced at the book. "Then scouting for Mr. Right?"

"Sure. And I always make a quick check of the local
libraries on my way home," she snapped back. "The
fact is, until about four this afternoon I was a model."

"What happened at four?"

"I turned idle but poor—which makes your cracks
about my status way off base."

His expression cleared slightly. When she turned angrily toward the kitchen, he dropped the books and
reached for the grocery bag, holding it as hostage. "I'm
sorry."

She faced him again. "You should be."

"No excuse except for the jitters."

"You? Jittery? The man with the yard-long line?"

His dark gaze riveted her. "I'm not used to fishing
this far out of my depth."

She knew he wasn't referring to her family's summer
house or to the decorator gloss of her apartment. The
pull between them was so real it felt like another presence in the room—one that was swirling them forward
too fast, growing too potent too soon. And the knowledge that he was heading halfway across the country
in a short while didn't help. Where would they find
time to learn to trust each other? Even ordinary rela-
tionships often went wrong. But there was nothing

ordinary about his effect on her, and the hours they had together were so few. Too few to waste.

She took a deep breath. "What do you say we scratch this last bit? Start over. Pretend this is normal—like being matched by a computer."

"Somebody sure juiced that computer," he said, but he relaxed enough to laugh. "If you had turned me down at the library, I planned to track you home and camp on your front sidewalk until you took pity on me."

"When the cops arrested you for loitering?"

"With intent. Definitely with intent. I figured there wasn't much risk. One look at you and they'd be on my side."

Her color rose. "Wouldn't it have been simpler to copy down my address—"

"And deluge you with fan mail from the wilderness? I thought about that, but there's a major drawback: I'd be there—and you'd be hundreds of miles away."

"That *would* be a problem," she said softly.

"I was so busy figuring out how to keep you from slipping away, I never gave a thought to what might happen if you accepted."

"Why does that sound so ominous?"

"Don't get me wrong. Half of my brain is crowing over my good fortune. I wouldn't exchange today for the past thirty years put together. It's just that—"

When he broke off, her heartbeat quickened. On romance covers an expression like the one on his face signaled a crisis of ravaged yearning. She half expected him to dump the groceries and sweep her into his arms. Instead the look clouded over while he ran his free hand through his hair in obvious frustration.

"A blind man could have told you were special," he said, "but I didn't guess *how* special."

"What do you mean?"

"Our worlds are so different, Nita. Glitz and glamour fit you like a dress you pulled out of your closet. I've spent more of my life in the woods than on paved streets. Until I saw New York, I thought *Chicago* was an asphalt jungle. There seems more ostentation in success here. I get the feeling everybody's fueling some colossal money machine that's simply going to turn around and gobble them up like a snake eating its own tail."

"Didn't we agree not to talk about money?"

"I owe you some kind of explana—"

"But you're *not* explaining," she interrupted. "You're trying to line me up along those tracks that divide the haves from the have-nots. I admit my experiences probably haven't been the same as yours. One of the ways they differ, though, is that I've never found places had monopolies on certain types of people. It isn't fair to sum me up by where or how I live as though I were a statistic in a market analysis."

Distress furrowed the strong planes of his face. "I'm off base again, aren't I?"

"Yes."

"I've already said I'm sorry. Can you make it double? Somehow simply standing near you triggers a bunch of antiquated defense mechanisms in me, as well as high blood pressure. Must be lack of oxygen to the brain."

"Sounds more like a nervous disorder."

"But is there a cure?"

She gave in and smiled. "More practice."

"Think so?" His grin deepened. "I'd like to test your theory out."

Dinner lasted long in the cooking and longer in the eating. They talked and joked nonstop, partly from the curiosity for detail that comes with a powerful attraction and partly to fend off silences that would say even more. By the time they rose from the table, cleaned up the kitchen, and carried brandy glasses into the living room, the ways Matt disturbed Nita had more to do with his allure than with any difference in their backgrounds. She'd told him half her life story, and the bits he'd revealed of his own were enough to make her decide gut reaction could be a better judge of compatibility than she'd imagined.

Baseball they'd both played from childhood. A love of

folk music and a shared enthusiasm for Garrison Keillor's tales from Lake Wobegon came later, along with shared awe at the majesty of the Great Lakes in all weathers and an enjoyment of family traditions. She had more than her share of anecdotes to tell. Hers was a fiercely knit clan.

"Of course, my brother Russell masterminded the whole scheme," she said, chuckling over the conclusion to one of those narratives as she settled back into the downy softness of the couch, her brandy snifter in her hand. "The twins' dates were due to spend the weekend at the cottage, so he rigged up some Rube Goldberg contraption to make the sides of the outhouse collapse if anyone pulled the chain. He even had a flag unfurl at the critical moment. It was a sensation. We all howled, except Cookie, of course, because her boyfriend was the one who got caught, and he drove off in a terrific huff without waiting for dinner—never to be heard from again."

"A chain flush in an outhouse?"

"No flush. Just the chain. That was the beauty of it. Actually, I think Aunt Addy kibitzed. She's a great believer in testing people for common sense."

"Sounds like a dangerous family."

"Meeting them is supposed to screen out all but the lionhearted." Frowning slightly, she rolled the snifter back and forth in her hands. "In practice, it seems to screen out everybody."

"Does that bother you?"

"Some."

"But you're not lowering your standards?"

She looked at him. "No."

He drained his glass, set it down on the table, and leaned back with his left hand millimeters from hers. Silence tightened around her so that she grew conscious of the muffled sounds of traffic in the street below, the refrigerator purring in the kitchen, the sudden racing of her heart. His little finger brushed back and forth, grazing the edge of her hand.

"I've been trying to decide," he said at last, "how to

leave before I put my elbows in my mouth along with both feet."

"Leave?" She stared at him, too astonished to do more than echo that word. Although she hadn't known what to expect next—anything from poetry to a sudden lunge of passion seemed plausible—the idea that he might just get up and walk out had never occurred to her.

"It must be pretty obvious I don't know how to handle the way I react to you."

"You don't?" She bit her lip. "I mean, you do?"

"This is a crazy setup."

"I know."

"I already want way too much for the time we have."

What he meant by too much she didn't even try to fathom. Still, the realization that the right person's finger tracing a path along her hand could upset all her notions about erogenous zones made it easy to think of a dozen things she wanted.

"You don't . . . really have to leave tonight?"

"I'm due at the college by eight on Monday. About fifteen minutes into dinner I gave up the idea of sleeping between now and then and spent the rest of the meal calculating how fast I dared push a geriatric Pontiac."

"You did think about staying?"

He laughed. "It crossed my mind."

"All that without missing a conversational beat? I bet you'd be a whiz if you ever tried logical problem solving."

"Travel time isn't the real problem."

Her heart seemed to clench. Then what was? Dire possibilities crowded her imagination: he not only disapproved of city life, he was a Communist opposed to her lifestyle in principle; he had a wife and three children waiting for him in Houghton. The last was likely enough. Life didn't scatter unattached men on every corner in the freehanded manner of romances. There was always some catch to send a person back to the book rack for another healing story.

"Hit me with the real problem," she said. "I'm tough."

The movement of his hand stopped, and if she needed proof of how important he'd become to her, the panic triggered by his pause would have given it in abundance. But he shook his head. "If you were tough, I would have carried you into the bedroom an hour ago."

Color poured into her face. "I might have survived."

"I wasn't sure I would."

"Why not?"

"I think I'm falling in love with you."

Nerves that had been stretched like rubber bands snapped with relief. Since when was falling in love a problem? "Could be worse," she said in a smothered voice.

"I knew you'd laugh."

"I'm sorry. It's just that everything is so . . ."

"Sudden? That's the understatement of the century. This is the damnedest thing that ever happened to me. One minute I'm carrying on an ordinary existence and the next I meet a woman so unlike anyone I ever expected to know that my world stops making sense. All my parameters are gone. Any idiot would realize nothing could last between two people whose lives are as different as ours, yet I'm scared to death the whole fantasy will disappear if I make the wrong move."

"Wouldn't leaving qualify as a wrong move?"

He hesitated, his hand clenched into a fist. "It's the only way to keep some elementary sanity. Already I'm holding onto every minute as though the time we have together were a saucer of milk I might spill."

"You're not the only one."

"Every man you meet is guaranteed to go around the bend within the first half-hour?"

"I meant I know how you feel."

"Sure you do." His laughter sounded painful. "Love at first sight. Dazzled by my affluence, my powerful connections. Swept off your feet by my finesse. Any clichés I missed?"

"What about 'opposites attract'?"

"If that's true, I'm a goner."

"But our feelings *aren't* different, Matt. That's what I'm trying to make you understand."

His gaze held hers for an endless moment before he flung himself forward with his hands clasped as though he couldn't trust them not to reach for her of their own volition. "Don't look at me like that. I gambled that telling you would put the craziness of the whole situation into some kind of perspective. I didn't bargain on making it harder than ever to let go."

"Then don't," she said softly. "I mean, don't go."

Two

Matt smiled wryly. "You're not making this easy."

"Look, we have—what?—maybe twenty-four hours before you *really* have to leave?" Nita spread her hands in a gesture of frustration. "All I want is a chance to figure out what's going on with us—with me—before you vanish."

"You mean, if I really cared, I'd stay?"

"Sounds good."

"Give me a break, Nita. We're not talking about whether I want time with you. I want it so badly it's frightening. I thought models knew something about body language. Can't you tell I'm practically sitting on my hands to keep them off you?"

"Then what *are* we talking about?"

"My family versus yours, for one thing."

Her eyes widened. "Are you serious?"

"Yes," he said grimly. "That's why it matters. Your relatives might consider a college professor marginally respectable. They'd probably prefer someone with an international reputation who teaches at Princeton or Harvard, but the work's steady and at least they wouldn't have to worry about me eating with my fingers in front of their friends. But where I come from I'm the big success, a phenomenon who slogged his way through something more elegant than a stint in the military or a chemical dependency program. In a town where half the adults exist from one welfare check to the next, I'm a hero."

"Oh, come on! Life in Houghton isn't that tough."

"I'm not talking about Houghton, Nita." The muscles in his jaw clenched and unclenched before he added, "After my parents split, my mother took my brother and me back to her home. I grew up in a spot in Canada so small it hardly makes the map. There's nothing up there but trees and water. It's like another world. You could hike for days in any direction without seeing a telephone pole or a dog you didn't know. By comparison my life in Houghton is the big time. Houghton." His laugh was humorless. "If the copper mines hadn't gone bust, it would be spewing smoke and people like Chicago does now. Makes me wonder whether anyone knows what the answers are."

"What are you talking about? You ought to be *proud* of what you've accomplished. I would be."

"Not if you saw the people you grew up with—and their parents and their kids—floundering in circumstances that get worse every year instead of better. I might have something to be proud of if I could turn the setup in that town around."

"And you think I couldn't sympathize?"

"You might understand it intellectually, but the kind of deprivation I'm talking about is totally foreign to you. How could you know how men feel who can't feed their families because pollution has shut down the fishing camps where they used to guide? You define poverty as losing a job worth a couple of hundred thousand a year! You've never been in the position of having no status, no social identity, because you have no meaningful occupation and no hope of getting one."

"But that's their problem," she exclaimed, "not yours."

"That's part of what you don't understand. It *is* my problem. The best of who I am is tied up with those people—that place—along with the worst. There's no way I can separate the two." He raised his eyes to study her face. "It's strange to talk to you like this. I'm probably the first Lamartine since my father's family left France to share a sofa with a woman who radiates self-assurance like a three-hundred-watt bulb."

"So what's wrong with that?"

"Wrong?" He shook his head. "Nothing's wrong.

There's not a false note in you. A couple of hours ago I would have sworn someone like you was a sociological impossibility, but you're exactly what you seem to be: spontaneous, frank, full of life. Everything's right about you." He paused. "That's what's wrong."

"I can't believe I'm hearing this!"

"Nita, there's no way for me to keep a woman like you."

"We're not deciding to get married!"

"You see?" His fist rammed into his palm. "For you this is no more than a quirky encounter. I caught you off stride, like a freak wind or a squall you weren't expecting. Next week you'll find a new job and forget you ever laid eyes on me."

"I could write Matt Lamartine in block letters all over my appointment book—starting with tomorrow."

"And ending when?"

"What do you expect? A written contract? I'm surprised you aren't worried about what our grandchildren will look like."

His grin resurfaced for an instant. "Brown eyes dominate."

"Are you like this with everyone? Planning your whole life in advance?"

"Hardly. I'm about as stable as a migratory bird. This seems to be a special occasion."

"Lucky me."

Hunched over her glass, she swirled the amber liquid. Bolts of lighting always sounded great in her romances. What had she done to make hers turn out like this? After zooming straight toward page one hundred eighty-two, their relationship seemed headed for a different genre altogether.

"Wild geese mate for life," he said slowly. "Did you know that?"

"Quit changing the subject."

"I wasn't."

She stared at him. He made it sound as though they *were* deciding to get married. After knowing her how many hours? Surprise stopped her cold—although *cold* wasn't the word to describe how she felt. Or the heady atmosphere around them.

"You could kiss me," she said, swallowing hard. "Just as an experiment. Maybe we'll both walk away free and clear."

"Do you believe that?"

"Not . . . exactly."

"Neither do I."

"So where does that leave us?"

"I guess it leaves me wanting something I can't have— and wanting it more than I did before."

He wasn't the only one, she thought. She hadn't run across a situation like this since fifth grade when she used to read love stories under the covers about chaste knights and ladies who slept with swords between them. How had she managed to meet the last romantic in the Western Hemisphere? Someone who treated a kiss more seriously than most men treated an affair? Who thought he ought to leave *because* he wanted to stay? If she had any sense, she'd point him toward the door. The man might be one of a kind, but who needed his kind? An inner ache of yearning and disappointment told her who.

"Matt—"

"Don't say anything. What I have to do is hard enough already."

"I'd like to make it impossible."

"You've come way too close."

She drew in her breath sharply at his bone-crunching grip on her hand, then he quickly released her. The couch cushions gave slightly as he heaved himself out of his seat, leaving all his grace of movement behind.

"Better get going," he said. "When a man can't think straight, night driving's the next best thing to being out in the woods alone."

He stopped to collect his pack from the chair where he'd dropped it only hours before, and Nita snatched at straws. Couldn't he see how wrong his decision was for both of them? "Your letter," she exclaimed. "What about your letter?"

"Letter?"

"The reason you came to New York."

He looked dazed. "I'd forgotten all about it. Shows you what shape I'm in."

"I wouldn't want you to drive off before you made a copy for Libby. You could . . ." She hesitated, took a deep breath, then set down her glass. "You could stay over in my spare room tonight. No strings attached."

He groaned. "Don't tempt me, Nita."

"I'm not twisting your arm. I have some pride—less than I figured, but some. Enough to feel like a fool for begging you not to walk out of my life. This is it, though. I'm not asking again. Last chance before the freeway." She stood up, choosing a dramatic exit line over the threat of tears. "If you really want to go, then go, dammit. Now. Don't stand around waiting to see whether I'll cry."

He put out his arm to stop her before she reached the hall. Strain harrowed his face. "Nita, please. Don't take it like that. Look, I—"

She sniffled and glared at him. "No, you look. I'm not promising anything. I'm not talking about forever. How could I? We're practically strangers! But you haven't any right to cut off my options without giving whatever this is a chance."

"You've no idea what's involved."

"No, I don't. That's the point. I want to!"

"But you—"

"Don't try to protect me, Matt. I'm not afraid of taking risks for someone special. I think you are and how you got that way doesn't matter a damn."

"I wish I believed that."

"Couldn't you try? Couldn't you trust me? Just a little?"

The tip of his index finger touched away the drop of moisture trembling in her lashes before it overflowed. "Hey, none of that," he murmured in a husky voice. "Unfair advantage."

"You didn't answer me."

"What about those family standards?"

She managed a tiny smile. "Just be glad Chicago's an easier trip from Houghton than New York."

"So far I must have failed your aunt's test for common sense about forty times."

"At *least*. But maybe they'll be crazy about you. Nobody could claim you're just like all the others."

"I still have to leave tomorrow."

Their gazes met, and longing fairly shimmered in the air around them. "Oh, come on, Sir Galahad," she said, seizing his arm, "tomorrow's soon enough to worry about tomorrow. The bath alone is worth staying for. I've practically cornered the market on chrome."

When she opened the bathroom door, he raised his brows at the lavish gym equipment in one corner. It had been her sole contribution to Dodie Kazjanian's design. "Lucky for me you didn't twist my arm," he said.

"You can sleep in the room next door. Mine is across the hall. I mention the location for information only."

"In case of fire."

"In case," she said, looking him squarely in the eye and planting a yellow-tipped finger in the center of his chest, "of anything."

Propped up on a wealth of pillows, Nita stared at the first page of the romance she'd chosen at random from the stack beside her bed. The shower running in the bathroom made reading impossible. With the real thing no more than fifteen feet away, how could fiction have its usual appeal?

The water stopped. An exploratory creak of the weight-lifting machine was followed by a seemingly endless silence. Finally the door scraped open over the thick carpet. Holding her breath, she strained to imagine Matt's movements. Would he come to her? What would she do if he did? Still, by now she knew him well enough not to expect him to act as most men would in this situation. Despite the inviting crack of light around her door, the man with the iron will would head straight for his room. She faintly heard a second door swish open.

She dropped her book with a sigh, switched off her

light, and scrunched down under the covers, but darkness failed to soothe her overactive brain. She pictured his head cradled by the pillow, his sinewy torso relaxing at last on the cool sheets. What would a man like Matt Lamartine wear to bed? Jockey shorts? Nothing at all? The possibilities weren't calculated to calm her imagination.

Her mattress pad twisted into ridges as she shifted from one side to the other. Suffocated by her quilt, she pushed it away, flopped her pillow over to its cooler side, and wondered whether the heating system had broken down. It must be over ninety degrees in her room. Matt was probably counting the hours until he could head for the cool north woods.

The thought of his departure snapped her eyes wide open. What could she say or do to change his mind tomorrow? He probably wouldn't buy a sudden revelation that she'd been found on the Holiday doorstep in a wicker basket. Bankruptcy was her other option. Too bad making money was the major talent in her family. Five minutes of conversation with them would have Matt expanding his estimate of the gulf between his lifestyle and hers to the size of the Grand Canyon.

She shuddered and pulled the covers close again for comfort. As long as Matt believed people were hostages to their past, what future could they make together? She was up against her own gilt-edged background, the Canadian and American social structure, and probably the whole free-enterprise system. Barriers in a romance were a test of true love, but this was ridiculous.

Determinedly, she sat up and plucked her robe from the chair beside her bed. Bags under her eyes wouldn't make her irresistible tomorrow. Time to try one of Uncle Bo's milk remedies for insomnia. If his recipe didn't put her to sleep, Aunt Addy's would.

Tiny bubbles were breaking the milky surface around the edge of the saucepan when Matt appeared in the kitchen doorway. Whatever he had worn or not worn to bed, he'd donned jeans for her benefit. His bare chest, however, displayed an expanse of hard muscle covered by smooth skin, whose bronze color would make any patron of a tanning parlor weep with envy. Her fingers ached to explore every burnished centimeter.

"Can't you sleep either?" she asked.

"Funniest thing."

She gestured from the pan of milk to the bottle of bourbon standing beside it. "I can offer you a choice between my Uncle Bo's favorite nightcap or Aunt Addy's."

"Actually, when I heard you up, I came to offer you a proposal of my own. If you'd as soon talk as count sheep, why don't you bring your drink down the hall to my place?" He revealed the blanket he'd been holding behind his back. "I'll even throw in a spare blanket."

Self-denial wasn't high on Nita's list of virtues. She was rummaging in the cupboard for a mug before he finished his sentence. "Be there in a sec."

When she entered the softly lit room, he was stretched out on the bed, his dark head pillowed on clasped hands, his gaze fixed on the ceiling. Whatever he'd been thinking left a gleam in his eyes when he turned toward her.

To compensate for giving in to temptation at the first opportunity, she perched on the extreme edge of the bed. He rose on one elbow to watch her slide out of her slippers. Drawing up her knees, she made an impromptu table for her mug of cinnamon-spiced milk. "What brought on the change of heart?"

"A cold shower," he said with a fleeting grin. "It didn't eliminate my basic problem, but it cleared my head."

"So you decided not to waste the time we have "

"Right."

She sipped her sweetened milk, but the warmth she felt was contentment. Their plot line had found its proper track. "Okay," she said, smiling. "If you think your life story is too hair-raising for bedtime, I'll settle for an account of what a professor does all day. I bet you constantly have a throng of girls waiting outside your office, all yearning to become mining engineers."

"Yup. They're crazy about our field trips—those thirty-mile hikes with full packs and twelve-hour days crouched over sample pans."

"Followed by nights under the stars?"

"Those are reserved for women with very special qualifications: only blondes with incredibly blue eyes that come exactly level with my mouth and who also have long, narrow feet." His hand reached out to curve so gently around her exposed toes she felt his touch only as a clutch of longing in the pit of her stomach. "Nobody younger than . . . Did you tell me how old you are?"

"No. It's a sore point today. Harrison—that's my agency—is letting me go because I'm past my prime."

"Who runs the place? Blind men?"

"One very sharp-eyed female." She was more conscious of the novel sensation of his hand around her foot than the logic of their conversation. "For a model, twenty-five is old age. I've been living on borrowed time. The minute photographers lose interest in someone and bookings start to drop, the agency gives them the boot."

"Nice business."

"I'll probably be just as tough when I'm running mine."

He traced her ankle bone with his thumb. "That's hard to believe."

"I don't plan to be *brutal*. For a couple of hours today I felt as though leaving the agency meant the end of the world. I don't really have such a cast-iron ego, you know, and the whole process was more threatening because I've been selling my looks instead of talent or expertise. Looks aren't supposed to improve with age." She hadn't forgotten her anxiety, but at this moment her concentration centered so completely on the few square feet of mattress they shared, talking about modeling was like talking about another life. "Since this afternoon I've had more on my mind than wrinkles."

"Handy I came along."

Something in his tone made her glance at him in surprise. "You know it was more than that."

"Was it?"

"Now wait a minute," she said. "Don't you take that chip off your shoulder even to sleep? I'm not sitting here because I want you to soothe my vanity. That's not why I couldn't sleep, why all my corpuscles crowd to share the excitement of your slightest touch, why I love to listen to you talk. Sure, losing my job was a shock; I thought I had more time. But I don't need a man in my life because I can't handle it."

"Then you must have plans."

"I always expected to go on my own."

"You mean start an agency?"

The wary edge was back in his voice and his hand released her foot. They were on dangerous ground again. She set her chin stubbornly. "My family has a talent for making money. I'm not going to apologize for having it too. For five years I traded on my face. Now I'll just have to think harder."

"So you're serious about your own business."

"I am. But nothing's set in concrete. Look, don't you think we've said enough for one night about money, my family, success in New York, and all the other reasons why you're so certain our relationship is doomed? You are not a specialist in the mindset of an ex-model who happens to have the bad luck to come from upper-class Chicago, and I don't need your advice on how to run my life at three in the morning." She took a deep breath and added in a milder tone, "Besides, I don't want to go back to my room with worse insomnia because we quarreled."

"We aren't going to quarrel. You choose the topic."

She studied her cup as though the secret of their future could be read in its depths. When she sought his eyes, she said softly, "Tell me about the woods. I've never slept in a sleeping bag, much less out under the stars. Tell me what it's like living that way every summer. Tell me why it means so much to you."

"That's a tall order. Once I get going, I'm good for hours."

"Do you mind?"

"Not for you." He took her mug and placed it on the bedside table, then lay back against the pillows. The husky timbre returned to his voice. "I even have a spare arm if you'd like to make yourself comfortable for a long-winded explanation."

Put in those terms, long-winded offered so many alluring features she didn't hesitate. The curve of his arm yielded a place along his long body, into which she curled as though she had always belonged there. Lightly resting her palm over his steadily beating heart, she closed her eyes and let his voice flow over her.

When Nita woke the next morning, she dimly remembered Matt's words dwindling to a distant murmur and covers being tucked around her limp body. She had dreamed of standing on the shore of a vast body of water, the piney fragrance of the woods filling the air around her.

"Finally decided to wake up?"

She turned her head. Barechested and barefooted, Matt was lounging against the doorway, smiling at her.

"What time is it?" she asked.

"Two."

"Two! You let me sleep until two in the afternoon?"

"Only fair after I wore you out."

She sat up, surreptitiously checking her surroundings for signs of former occupancy. He laughed. "I slept in your room."

"A whole morning wasted!"

"Not totally. Your sheets smell like you."

Her color rose, but she bit her lip and flung back the bedclothes. "You must be starved."

"Just about."

"Breakfast coming up!"

Neither of them mentioned his departure. She avoided the words as though he might vanish if they were spoken. Yet everything persuaded her it couldn't happen: his bursts of off-key song in the shower while she skimmed through her morning exercise routine, the way his gaze followed her around the kitchen as she made toast and scrambled eggs, the ease with which silence and talk had begun to blend. They were right together. Nothing else was going to matter.

Sun filtered through the blinds to streak his hair as they sat down to eat. "You look as chipper as the first yellow crocus," he said, grinning at her across a steaming cup of coffee.

"Having company agrees with me."

"Everything agrees with me."

"Changing your opinion about city life?"

He laughed. "Keeping an open mind. What would you be doing right now if I weren't here?"

Determined not to think about his absence or to glance at the clock, she wrinkled her nose. "Jogging. And trying to figure out a way to prove there's life after the Harrison Agency."

"Aren't there other agencies?"

"Harrison is the best. Modeling's no picnic, especially if you're doing it for peanuts. I'd rather work for myself than pose for underwear ads."

"That means capital."

"Appearances to the contrary, I've been saving."

He stared down at his coffee as he stirred sugar into it. "But not enough?"

"Before I answer, is money still a dangerous subject?"

When he looked at her, she caught a flash of intensity she'd previously associated only with his Jesuit project. Could a person become reconciled to capitalism overnight?

"Tell me," he said carefully, sugaring his coffee a second time. "I'm interested."

"Well then, yes, probably enough for a start. The basic problem is that I haven't zeroed in on a business angle yet. Fashion seems the most logical thing. Seemed," she added hastily, in case he thought she was determined to stay in New York. A spoon could have stood up by itself in his cup, but he downed its contents without seeming to notice.

"Ever consider investing?" he asked.

"No," she answered with a grin. "I keep my money in a sock under my mattress."

"I'm serious, Nita. Have you thought of using what you've saved as venture capital? Backing someone?"

His question was so unexpected she simply stared at him. "Backing someone in what?"

"Gold."

"Oh, come on! Do you think I'm as gullible as I look?" She shrugged and added, "I keep a five-percent hedge in gold the same as everyone else. My sisters handle it for me. They run a newsletter on the gold market out of Monterey."

"You're joking."

"About money? Not in my family. We all practically cut our teeth on investments. Now Russell's taking over from Uncle Bo in real estate and the twins are into gold. By rights, I should be working on thoroughbreds like Aunt Addy." She smiled at him. "If you had a hot tip, that would be another story. Is Disney buying the whole Upper Peninsula?"

"You're close. In scale at least. Look, Nita, the study I was telling you about yesterday isn't abstract. There's a major gold lode in Ontario—east of Lake Superior—one nobody suspects. I've been collecting evidence for years. If this Jesuit lead pans out, I'll be ready to make a big push over the summer."

"Now who's joking?"

"All the pieces are falling into place," he continued, too intent on his explanation to acknowledge her interruption. "I'd wager anything you want to name that I could bring in a minable claim within six months. But finding backing's been harder than finding the vein. Canadians aren't keen on funding an American and the American agencies aren't interested in a mine site in Ontario."

A cold feeling stabbed at the pit of her stomach as she began to suspect what he had in mind. She sat back in her chair without relaxing a muscle. "So you think I'm an easy touch for a loan?"

"A *major* lode, Nita. Do you know what that would mean?"

"I have some idea," she said scornfully. "If there had been a prayer of mining gold anywhere around the Great Lakes, somebody would have done it before you were born!"

"Not the place I have in mind."

"Investing is one thing, but I'm not throwing money down a bunch of holes just as a speculation."

"Nita, for Pete's sake. I'm not peddling the Brooklyn Bridge!"

"And I'm not buying, either."

They glared at each other. The possibility that he had conceived this scheme in the grocery store and consolidated it when he saw her apartment hurt too much for her to contemplate.

"I wouldn't propose the idea if there were any risk," he said. "You'd get a percentage written into the contract. The money couldn't be safer in the bank."

"That line was ancient during the Gold Rush! Nobody but you would have the nerve to try a gold-mining scam in the twentieth century."

"Is that what you think?"

Her lower lip trembled. "What else can I think?"

"There's another possibility," he said slowly. "One that makes more sense to me. In spite of all your talk about keeping options open and giving this relationship between us a chance, as soon as I mention money everything changes. Suddenly I'm worse than an outsider—I'm some kind of crook."

"And I fell for your Sir Galahad routine!"

"I never told you anything I didn't feel." He shoved his plate aside impatiently. "You want to know what was on my mind while I was lying awake last night supposedly inventing ways to cheat you? I was thinking that when I found this lode we'd be even. I could come back for you and maybe, by some miracle, you'd still be free."

"I'll bet that wild goose story came to mind because you pictured me laying golden eggs!"

He reached out a hand. "Nita."

"Don't touch me."

"That's a switch."

"Did you think I couldn't change my mind?"

His face whitened under his tan, but his gaze held steady. "No," he said. "That's about what I expected."

In silence he stood up, caried his dishes to the sink,

and poured the dregs of his coffee down the drain. The three moles on his jaw stood out sharply, and the cold sensation in her stomach iced into a lump. "You're not leaving?" she asked.

"Seems as though I'm about ten or twelve hours overdue."

"I'm sorry about the offer, but—"

"Forget it. My mistake."

"You don't understand."

"That's where you're wrong," he said as she followed him into the living room. "I do understand." At the door he shrugged his knapsack on. "Maybe you want to check me out before I leave? Make sure I'm not sneaking off with any of the silver?"

"Matt—"

He shook his head. "Got to get moving. If you come north sometime, look me up. I'll take you sightseeing, show you how the natives live, maybe a mine shaft or two. I'm in the book."

"I'm not."

"That figures."

"It's not that late," she said haltingly. "We could talk about your idea some more . . ."

"Talk never solved anything."

"But we need more time."

He abandoned his grip on the doorknob long enough to reach out and tuck a strand of her hair behind her ear. "All the time in the world can't help if the main point's missing. Maybe you could take on a partner you didn't trust; I never felt like living or even working that way myself."

Their gazes held, but she couldn't argue with what he'd said. If trust was the main thing, they didn't have it. She swallowed. "So you won't stay?"

"It's a long trip. All the way back to reality."

A nod of farewell, then the heavy thud of the door shutting behind him echoed through the apartment. Leaning her head against the jamb, Nita closed her eyes and pictured him walking down the stairs, out into the street, and into a life she couldn't imagine.

So much for her bolt of lightning.

Laundry and dirty dishes didn't distract her. Nor did manicuring her nails, washing her hair a second time, or dressing. He must be upstate by now, she thought as she slipped on her shoes, heading toward those mythical fields of gold. Would they ever meet again?

Chores she normally wouldn't dream of tackling she took on with a fierce burst of energy. She cleaned closets that didn't need cleaning, scrubbed the kitchen and bathroom floors, experimented with starting a batch of sourdough. Probably he'd hit Cleveland sometime that night, then Toledo, eventually Detroit and Houghton. How many Matthew Lamartines could there be in one town?

After changing her clothes and nail polish for the second time, she was reduced to paperwork. Imagining whether his car was acting up, what time he might reach home, and in what state of mind so effectively distracted her from balancing her accounts that the same $3.23 mistake turned up first as $323.00 and then as $3,230.00. At that point she gave up, slung on a jacket, and headed for the West Side.

"Nita!" Libby cried as she opened her apartment door. "Don't tell me you've brought the letter already."

"What letter?"

Libby chuckled. "Then how'd it go?"

"He went."

"When?"

"A couple of hours ago."

"I was dying to call you, but I said, 'Hold on, friend, don't interrupt anything.' " Libby hung Nita's jacket in the hall closet and exclaimed, "You look great."

Nita grimaced. "Looks can be deceiving."

"Don't play casual with me. The two of you were obviously on the same wavelength last night. Come on into the kitchen and tell me all about him. I made coffee cake for breakfast and there's a tiny piece left."

"Domestic bliss. How can you stand it?"

"I'm thriving," Libby said, but a cloud crossed her face. "Am I getting fat?"

"Are you pregnant?"

"No, why?"

"You asked."

Libby groaned. "You really think I'm gaining weight?"

"Let's say I have a load of gym equipment I may be selling cheap."

"You know we haven't room for—" Libby paused and gave Nita a suspicious look. "Are you avoiding telling me something? Did you change your mind about him?"

"Not . . . exactly."

"So you're going to keep in touch, right?"

"Depends," Nita said glumly.

"On what?"

"Let me put it this way. How do you see gold as an investment?"

Libby laughed. "As if I'd give you advice."

"Matt thinks he's found a gold mine near Lake Superior."

"What's that got to do with anything?"

"He wants me to back him."

"Hunting for gold in the middle of nowhere? You're putting me on. . . ." Libby's smile faded. "Aren't you? I mean, talk about crazy pipe dreams! Or are visions of striking it rich an occuptional hazard for mining engineers?"

"I don't know any other mining engineers, but he's plenty serious." Nita scowled into her cup. "How much do you think it would cost to start up a mine?"

"You're not considering it, are you?"

"I'd get a percentage."

"Of what?"

"Whatever there was."

"Don't be absurd. A hundred percent of zero is still zero. You're not going to let someone con you into prospecting for gold!"

"I'm not?"

"Oh, my gosh, is that the way you feel about him?"

Nita's necklaces jangled under her friend's impetuous hug. "What a rotten shame," Libby added, her face full of concern. "Even though he's not the type you usually date, I thought maybe the change was a good thing. I just can't believe all he had in mind . . . I mean, he seemed so . . . so . . ."

"He was."

"Have some coffee cake."

Nita pushed away the offered plate. "This is not a problem to handle with food. Just listen to me for a minute. Let's look at all the possibilities before we reject the idea out of hand. Calmly and rationally. No preconceptions, no emotional influences. There are reasons why it might not be such a dumb move."

Libby sighed. "Falling in love makes women irrational."

"Some women."

"Look at you—"

Ticking off points on her fingers as she went, Nita ignored the interruption. "Reason one: The man's a mining engineer, a doctor of something-or-other, not a two-bit prospector. Reason two: He's been working on this project for years and he's too bright to waste his time on a dud scheme. Reason three: The timing is right. I was planning to start some kind of business eventually, and Harrison has decided the time is now. Reason four: We have complementary skills. I have the management ability, he has the technical ability. The perfect partnership. Reason five: If we found the mine, he'd feel we were on the same economic footing. No more paranoia about the haves against the have-nots. Reason six—"

"Never mind reason six. You've made up your mind already, haven't you?"

"Of course not. I'm simply thinking out loud."

"Rationally?"

"You know me."

Libby laughed and sat back in her chair. "That must be why it took me so long to catch on. If one of my *emotional* friends had turned up with prospecting on the brain and wearing a yellow silk shirt, five gold chains, a pair of gold cuff bracelets, gold rings, and gold nail polish, I'd have guessed what was going on in a minute."

Staring first at Libby, then down at her chest and hands, Nita groaned. "Oh, Lord."

"Pretty obvious, huh?"

"You think I'm crazy?"

Her friend's brown eyes twinkled. "I think you two talked about more than mining."

"Mmm." Nita's voice drifted off as she remembered. "Geese."

"What?"

"Wild geese."

Libby chuckled. "I can see why you fell for him. Perfectly normal. Anyone would react the same way. Geese are so sexy."

"Okay." Nita wrenched herself out of her reverie. "Cut the comedy. Do I still have time to get to Rare Books?"

"I think so."

"I'll be back with a copy of the letter. Can you start transcribing tomorrow?"

Libby smiled. "I'll try."

At six-thirty in the morning Nita was sitting up in her bed, clutching the phone. As she had done every fifteen minutes for the last three hours, she was punching in the Houghton, Michigan, number for Matthew Lamartine. And, as they had done each time before, her heart pounded and her palm grew sweaty around the receiver while she listened to the rings.

"Lamartine."

His voice took her breath away for an instant.

"Hello? Hello!"

"You're home," she gasped, winning another prize for witty dialogue. He didn't seem to notice.

"Nita? Where are you?"

"In bed." Did the same image flash into both their minds? she wondered. Through the silence she could hear him breathing. Her voice gentled to a husky murmur. "When did you get back?"

"Just walked in the door."

"You made good time."

"Old Pontiac decided I needed a break."

She hesitated. "Would you . . . like another?"

"Is this a business or a personal call?"

"Do you have a preference?"

"It's your bill."

She switched ears and hands, dried her palm on the bedclothes, and cleared her throat. "I guess we could call it business."

"Suit yourself."

"Matt?"

"I'm listening."

"Maybe we'd better call it personal."

The silence at the other end of the line made her wonder whether they'd been cut off. Finally he said, "I'm still listening."

"I've . . . been thinking about the offer you made. It sounds better now that the shock's worn off."

"And?"

"I might be able to help."

"I wasn't asking for favors."

Damn, she thought. He wouldn't let her off easily. The chip on his shoulder hadn't shrunk any on his trip north. "I meant, maybe we could make a deal."

"You've decided to speculate?"

"I . . . heard there was a good man in charge."

"The kind who's hard to find?"

"Yes."

"You're sure?"

"Yes."

More silence. Was he deciding how far to trust her? Or wondering how high a price he dared name? Unnerved, she exclaimed, "There probably isn't as much money as you think, but I have some ideas about how we might raise the rest."

"Already planning to take over?"

"So who doesn't trust who?"

"Whom."

"Oh, Lord, the professor speaks."

His laughter broke then, deep and full. "I missed you. I slowed down at the end because I couldn't face an empty apartment."

"There's one here too."

"It's a bum arrangement."

"We might be able to work out another." She hurried

on, afraid he'd contradict her or she'd lose her nerve. "When is your term over?"

"Mid-May."

"Come to Chicago."

"You mean meet your family?" He sounded cautious.

"You could count it as a trip to solicit backers and take it off your taxes."

"Where does the business come in?"

"We'll work up a consortium. A tribal council. I hope you realize you have hooked up with one smart partner, Mr. Lamartine. Tiny bosom, but giant brain. You come to Chicago, give my family a sensational pitch, and they kick in the rest of the funds we need."

"So if the mine makes money . . . ?"

"They'll go nuts over you. Nothing will be too good. No doubt about it. What do you think? Sensational, isn't it? Can we do business?"

She snuggled deeper into her bed, her eyes closed, willing the response she wanted. And the warmth of his laughter swelled out to envelop her. "I think," he said, "you just made me an offer I can't refuse."

Three

Three weeks and many long-distance phone calls later, Nita stood shivering beside the floodlit granite pillars at the entrance to her aunt and uncle's condominium complex. Gusts driving shoreward off Lake Michigan plastered her thin dress against the backs of her legs and blew her hair forward like a banner. Typical Windy City welcome, she thought. A pile of suitcases grew steadily on the curb beside her brother's car as he and two doormen unloaded the paraphernalia she carried on all her trips.

"Coldest May fifteenth on record," Russell yelled across to her with satisfaction. "If it goes down to twenty-eight before midnight, I win fifty bucks from everybody in the pool."

"And if it doesn't?"

A frown temporarily clouded her brother's blond good looks. "Then I owe them."

"Easy come, easy go," Nita said with a grin, but the wind's bite took on a new significance for her. If Russell felt flush and lucky, he'd be more responsive to Matt's proposal. Flush seemed to be no problem. All the way from the airport she'd been regaled with details about Russell's latest real estate coup, a deal giving him a forty-year break in property taxes on a new hotel site in Chicago's Loop. The only blight on his triumph was not being able to put his own name on the building, as Donald Trump had done with Trump Tower in New York. "If I called it Holiday Tower," Russell had complained, "people would think I'd built a fancy Holiday Inn." Maybe he'd settle for Holiday Mines.

With her luggage finally loaded on a dolly and headed for the elevator, Nita paused at the porter's desk. "I'll be expecting a guest tomorrow," she said, still snagging fine strands of hair back from her face. "His name's Matthew Lamartine."

"Sure thing, Miss Holiday. Good to see you again."

"New sheep to the slaughter?" Russell asked when the elevator door closed behind them.

"Just lay off him when he gets here, okay? No hotfoots, no frenched beds."

"Hey, give me some credit. I'm into technology now. Stuff like ethyl chloride. One squirt'll freeze your hair so it cracks right off."

"When are you going to grow up?"

"After waiting until I was twenty-nine to become a boy genius? But I'm hot now, honey, I'm hot. Women are crawling all over me. They can sniff out success the way dogs sniff out cocaine."

Nita grimaced. "So what else is new?"

As the doors slid open at the penthouse level, Russell winked at the young doorman over the baggage-piled dolly. "Wait'll you meet Gloria. She's coming to the party tomorrow."

"What party?" Nita's heart sank. A quiet dinner would have eased Matt's introduction to the family. "Nobody mentioned a party."

"Only about a hundred people. To celebrate the hotel deal," Russell said nonchalantly. "You're going to love this girl. What a sense of humor! The other day I kept her waiting in the office while I was on the phone, and you know what she did?"

"I hate to think."

"Stapled my tie onto my desk! Right into the mahogany."

"A real wit."

Flipping open the apartment door, Russell added, "But this is the kicker. You know how she did it? In the shape of a heart. Cute, huh?"

"Sounds as if you two are made for each other."

"Yeah," Russell said thoughtfully. "Yeah."

The living room was empty except for Nita's twin sisters. Hidden behind open newspapers, they occupied the yellow-and-turquoise damask sofas like commuters on a train whose walls happened to be paneled with misty silken landscapes rather than shampoo ads. Although their given names were Lara and Leslie, almost everyone called them Sugar and Cookie. Those names were more easily associated with their aura of arrested prettiness. Nothing they tried—not smoking like chimneys at fifteen or stunning the market analysts at twenty-two—seemed to dispel a lingering image of sausage curls and fluffy dresses. As the doorman trundled Nita's luggage across the carpet toward the bedroom hallway, Cookie lowered her *Wall Street Journal.* "Your friend phoned," she said.

"Matt? When?"

Sugar's wheat-blond head emerged from behind the *New York Times.* "He called twice."

"I love those mellow baritones," Cookie added. "They give me goose bumps all over."

Russell guffawed, flung his lanky frame into a chair beside the gray marble fireplace, and helped himself to a fistful of chocolates from a bowl on the low table. "Anybody fill you in on the latest wrinkle in Holiday human relations yet, Ni?"

"What do you mean?" Nita asked.

"The twins are into marriage statistics. Came up with a real eye-opener right off the bat."

Cookie sat up straight. "Eighty percent of women over thirty never marry."

"And our thirtieth birthday is next December!" Sugar wailed.

"Really lit a fire under them," Russell said. "Place is turning into a damn frat house between the three of you. They invited some croquet champ—"

"Polo player," Sugar said indignantly.

"And I asked him first," Cookie added.

Nita groaned inwardly. The twins' threesomes had guaranteed squabbles even before they became marriage-minded. "About my phone call," she said. "Was there any message?"

Aunt Addy materialized near the living room liquor cabinet wearing a satin dressing gown that deliberately accentuated her resemblance to Helen Hayes. She acknowledged Nita's arrival by tilting her perfumed cheek for a kiss. "Message from whom, dear?"

"A friend of mine, Aunt Addy. He's coming here tomorrow."

"How nice." Her aunt poured a stiff nightcap. "Extra men are always so useful at a party."

"Matt's not exactly *extra*."

Aunt Addy sipped her bourbon as meditatively as though she were drinking dandelion wine. "Perhaps he could distract that gold digger of Russell's."

"Oh, hell!" Russell said.

"Don't swear, dear. That won't change a thing. You know what I said the first time you brought her to the apartment."

"Russell thinks Gloria's crazy about him—" Cookie said.

"Because nobody else laughs at his jokes," Sugar finished.

The plot was thickening too fast for Nita's taste. If the unknown Gloria stumbled on the right questions to ask Matt, she might be tempted to try gold digging in the most literal sense of the word. The twins' threesome could turn into mayhem for six.

"Did Matt tell either of you when he'd arrive?" she asked hastily.

"He was so cute on the phone," Sugar said.

"But what did he *say*?"

"He wanted to know whether we'd give him lessons on how to keep track of the gold market. And Cookie said of course we would since he was a friend of the family—"

Nita struggled for patience. "About his *flight*."

"He'll be at the airport at four-fifteen."

Cookie smiled sweetly. "We told him we'd be there."

"Now just wait a minute, all of you." Nita glared at

the deceptively guileless faces turned in her direction. "Since the subject has come up, I'd like to make one thing about this weekend clear. Matt Lamartine is *my* guest. I intend to meet him at the airport *alone*. And when I bring him back here, as a personal favor to me, will you kindly not harass him, arrange women for him to meet, or otherwise screw up my life?"

"I'm sure you needn't tell your own family how to behave," Aunt Addy said. The look in her eye made Nita nervous. "I hope your friend won't mind sharing a room."

Russell grinned. "Probably depends on whose."

"Why, Russell, dear, whatever do you mean? Unless you're offering to share yours, he'll have to go in with the polo player."

The twins groaned in unison.

Aunt Addy silenced them in her best Helen Hayes manner. "Well, you could hardly expect your Uncle Bo to share!"

One hardly could, although Nita felt a wild urge to ask her uncle when she met him carrying a glass of milk down the hall a few minutes later. "I'm having company for the weekend," she said, pecking his leathery cheek.

"How's his billiard game? The fellows you've brought round lately couldn't seem to handle anything more complicated than refilling their glasses."

"I'm not sure he plays, Uncle Bo."

"Ought to check 'em out."

"Aunt Addy didn't marry you for your billiard game."

"Ad married me to pay her folks back. They wouldn't let her try her luck at being a jockey, so she ran off with a sailor instead." He chuckled. "As a matter of fact, I didn't give her a chance to say no."

"It worked out better for you than for Mom and Dad," Nita said. "They were so busy avoiding each other after their divorce, if you hadn't taken the four of us in, we'd have grown up living in hotel rooms and swapping continents every six months."

"Oh, Ad and I pull together when it counts." He gave Nita a hard look. "You serious about this fellow, Ni?"

"I'm not giving him a chance to say no."

"Well, then," Uncle Bo said with relish, "he'd better play a damn sharp game."

Nita stood alone behind the rail that fenced off the arrival area at Midway airport, her knuckles whitening as she clamped both hands around the metal. Phone calls were all well and good, she thought, but what if the magic was gone when they saw each other again? In romances such things never happened, but real life was less kind.

The dark head at the rear of the crowd walking across the tarmac had to be his. Her heart started to thump. Her smile of welcome stiffened. Confronting the stranger whose voice she'd heard more often by phone than in person, yet who'd grown to be the first focus of her every thought, took all her courage. Suddenly she didn't know where to look and began to dart glances in all directions except the one from which he was approaching. But the stream of disembarking passengers opened up as though by design, and their eyes met.

She caught her breath, incapable of movement or speech, buffeted by the flow of people who parted to pass around her. Matt's pack hung over one shoulder and his hair curled slightly over the buff leather collar of his buckskin jacket. Buckskin jacket! An image of tonight's party for a hundred people flashed through her mind, along with the certain knowledge that Matt Lamartine didn't travel with a dinner jacket in his pack. But then all thought vanished as he stepped toward her. With a tiny cry she was in his arms, her nose pressed into the soft, creamy leather and her arms around his solid body. How could she have doubted it would be the same?

"How was your flight?" she asked, laughing with relief.

"Fine." He grinned down at her.

"It's great to see you."

"What is it about you that shrinks my vocabulary down to one or two words?"

"Like what?"

"*Wahoo* comes to mind first."

"At least it's appropriate. Look what came in the mail this morning." She fumbled in a shoulder bag far bigger and more heavily loaded than his pack. "Libby's transcription!"

Her head bent close to his. While he studied the papers, she snuggled in the crook of his arm, savoring his nearness, smiling at the fatal earlobe and the three moles marking the angle of his jaw.

"I think we've got it!" he said.

"The information you wanted?"

His smile broadened. Clasping her waist more tightly, he strode along the corridor with a swing of happiness in his gait. "Yup. Everything points in the same direction."

"Fantastic!"

"Lead me to your people," he said, laughing. "Now I can handle anything."

The thought of what awaited him made Nita swallow hard in spite of the euphoria she felt when she looked at him. "By the way, how's your billiard game?"

"Pro. Why?"

"Do you mean it?"

"One of the legacies of my misspent youth."

So far so good. Unless he beat Uncle Bo and ruined everything.

When he slid into the leather seat of Russell's Mercedes with no more comment than a raised brow, she decided his determination to keep a truce was too precious to endanger by mentioning the party just yet. Assembled status and money weren't the ideal welcome for someone who disapproved of "Chicago people."

He draped his arm across the back of the seat so that his fingertips grazed the knot of blond hair at the nape of her neck. "I've bought so many back copies of fashion magazines in the past three weeks, my place looks like a secondhand store, but none of your pictures compare with the original."

"I'm glad I'm not an anticlimax."

"Don't worry."

A spreading warmth of satisfaction made her decide not to hurry back to the apartment. As she detoured to show him the hundred-foot Claes Oldenburg sculpture of a baseball bat in all its meshwork glory, she kept the conversation to safe topics—Comisky Park versus Wrigley Field; Chisox' and Cubs' players she'd seen when she was a kid. No use taking unnecessary risks.

The day was cloudless and sparkling. Late afternoon sun gilded the city's towers and stretched a band of metallic glitter across the surface of the lake. Chicago had never looked better, but after an hour and a half of meandering around the city, the current of awareness between them finally shifted and broke. Nita tensed instantly.

"Are you marking time for some reason?" Matt asked.

"No." She cursed herself for flushing. "Why?"

"Because if you're trying to throw off my sense of direction, I still know which way is north."

She twisted her grip on the wheel. "I wanted some time alone with you before we went back. Do you mind?"

"Not if that's the only reason. A hunch says it isn't."

"My family's having a—a little get-together tonight. Russell's celebrating."

"Swell." He paused. "Or maybe too swell?"

"Actually, it won't be so little."

"Black tie?"

She nodded.

"And you're afraid I won't pass?"

"As if it were something as stupid as that!"

"I could always come as the Noble Savage."

She pulled into the curved drive of the condominium complex and stopped in front of the granite pillars, already miserable because of the edge in his voice. "The party tonight is a real foul-up and I'm sorry. You're going to hate it, considering the way you feel about people with money."

"You were hoping to postpone my arrival until the next stock market crash?"

"I'm glad you can joke about it."

"Stand-up comedy's my other talent. But no offensive material about the needy or underprivileged. I wouldn't want to offend my potential backers."

The doorman hurried forward to open the car door, and Matt's expression as he took in the facade of the building made her wince. "Okay, then," she said. "Welcome to Chicago."

"This is it?"

"Mmm. You're looking at prime Gold Coast property."

"It better earn its name," he said grimly.

They rode the elevator in silence. At least the whole clan hadn't assembled in the living room, Nita thought as they entered. Russell and Uncle Bo were alone. But since her uncle, who wasted no time on inconsequential talk, immediately invited Matt to see the billiard room before the crowd arrived, it was too late for warnings.

"Where's your friend's luggage?" Russell asked as Uncle Bo piloted Matt down the hall. "The twins decided to share, so Aunt Addy's given him the 'Rose Room.' Supposed to remind him of the great outdoors."

Nita tried to imagine Matt feeling at home in a bedroom swagged, tented, and ruffled in chintz printed with green-and-rose butterflies. "He's carrying his luggage," she answered distractedly.

Russell eyed her with surprise. "Kind of a switch in type for you, isn't he?"

"No wisecracks. Can you lend him some evening clothes?"

"And make it easier for Aunt Addy to palm him off on my girl? Gloria has a thing for dark-haired men anyway."

Nita groaned. "Look, Russell, I promise I won't let him out of my sight."

"Well, I wouldn't bet on you over Aunt Addy, but okay."

"Be tactful when you offer, will you? And no drop-seated pants?"

"Damn. I wish I'd thought of that."

When she knocked on Matt's door before she went to dress, he was swearing as he struggled to manipulate a collar stud. His image glared at her from the mirror. "I thought these gadgets went out with the flivver."

"Let me help."

He gestured toward the bed. "Your brother forgot the instructions when he dumped off this pile of stuff. As far as I can see, half of it's useless and the parts I've been able to figure out don't fit."

She grinned at him. "I've never seen you flustered."

"You mean, except by you? I feel as though I were putting on a damned disguise."

"Think of it as infiltrating the enemy camp."

"Don't laugh. See if you can keep this shirt from flapping open to the navel and shocking everyone in the place."

The expanse of chest displayed by his pleated shirt front might easily cause a sensation, Nita thought. She knew of at least three women who wouldn't regret the absence of shirt studs, but the effect was far too potent to let loose on Gloria or Cookie and Sugar. She picked sapphire studs from the neat pile on the bureau and inserted them one by one, the back of her hand pressing against his smooth, warm skin. She experienced a heady sensation that had nothing to do with the mixed fragrance of fresh after-shave and starched linen.

"This phase I might learn to tolerate," he said.

"You'd make an elegant rich man."

"Is that a condition?"

"The only conditions are in your own head."

"Are they?"

"Yes."

"I'd give ten years to believe you meant that."

Her gaze met his. The space between them shrank without conscious movement, and the tilt of her head brought her mouth within a breath of his. Longing choked her voice. "Can't you even trust me that much?"

"Trust you? You think I don't want to trust you? Oh, Nita, Nita, Nita . . ." He pulled her suddenly into a crushing embrace, burying his face in her hair with a groan so deep it seemed borne of weeks of pent-up desire. "Have you any idea how many times I've gone over every word we said that morning?"

"I know. So have I."

"I never felt this way about anyone before. You have to believe me. I was ready to grab a plane back to New York fifty times."

"Why didn't you?"

"Because I can't change what I am to fit into your world." His bitter laugh ruffled her hair. "You see how much trouble I have just changing my clothes."

"I don't want you to change." She nuzzled his shoulder, sampling the contour of muscle and sinew with her cheek. "I just want us to be good to each other. And I want you to hold me like this for a long, long time."

His grip tightened. "When can we get away?"

"Tomorrow sometime."

"I might never bring you back."

"Under the right circumstances," she murmured as she let her body lean more heavily against his, "I might not notice."

Suddenly the door burst open. "Have everything you need, Lamartine?" Russell asked. "Oops! Sorry! I guess you do."

Lifting her head, Nita struggled for enough presence of mind to draw away, as Matt released her. "Come on in, Russell. I . . . never could get the hang of tying a bow tie."

"Out of practice." He winked at Matt. "She's a whiz at everything else. Buttons, belt buckles. No problem on or off. I expect you've discovered that."

"Russell!"

"Can't you take a joke?" He looked aggrieved.

Matt didn't smile. "I'd appreciate a hand with this tie."

"No problem. Don't usually do it on other men, but I'll have you fixed up in a jiffy."

"I'd better dress too," Nita said. "See you later?"

"In full battle gear," Matt said.

"You're bound to be a sensation."

"One way or another."

"Russell's given me his word."

Her brother, somewhat sobered by Matt's impressive appearance in the clothes he had loaned him, muttered under his breath, "And I hope to hell you keep yours."

But Nita broke her promise to keep Matt at her side within the first fifteen minutes of the party. She caught a glimpse of him all right, and her brother's evening clothes had never looked so dramatic. Tanned skin set off the white shirtfront. The black jacket echoed his ebony hair, whose shaggy curl hinted at a nonchalance permissible only to the very rich or someone with Matt's craggy good looks. A million dollars wouldn't have added to the smoldering aura that clung to him. Clusters of guests near the doorway revolved in his direction when he appeared, and women all over the room came alive.

"Who is that wickedly attractive man, dear?"

Nita tore her gaze from Matt to focus on her aunt. "Matthew Lamartine."

Aunt Addy frowned. "Now where have I heard that name?"

"He's my friend from Houghton, Aunt Addy."

"I remember *that*. No, your uncle must have mentioned him. Evidently he's quite a billiard player. Well, I hope his appearance piques Gloria's interest."

"Aunt Addy, please!"

"Your friend seems quite capable of taking care of himself, dear. Not like your poor brother."

Her aunt headed purposefully in Matt's direction. Nita was about to follow when she was cornered by an old friend of her aunt's, who was determined to find out everything Nita had been doing in the past year. As she dutifully answered the older woman's questions, Nita lifted a gin and tonic from a passing tray of drinks. It looked as though it might be that kind of night. Musicians stationed near the French doors leading to the terrace segued into a new selection. Through a gap in the shifting press of bodies Nita could see Matt bending down to listen to Aunt Addy's request.

Ten minutes later Nita had satisfied her companion's curiosity and began slowly making her way through the crowd toward Matt. She had noted that fortunately

—or perhaps unfortunately—Cookie had been his constant companion, no doubt making up for time missed at the airport. Dressed in gray silk toreador pants, white hose, red pumps with filigree buckles to match her belt, and a serape strung with bangles, Cookie had fended off all but the women most determined to make Matt's acquaintance. Nita hoped Matt was using the opportunity to quiz Cookie about the international price of gold, but if her sister's rapt expression signified anything, market analysis was the furthest thing from her mind.

Russell threaded his way toward Nita, holding two plates loaded with lobster salad above the heads of his guests. "Met her yet?" he asked.

"Who?"

"Gloria."

"No, and you shouldn't let her out of your sight."

"I wouldn't, except Aunt Addy's had me running around like a caterer. Now she wants lobster salad."

"You could try putting Tabasco on everything."

His face lit up. "That's an idea. Say, your friend's all right. I tipped him off about Gloria. He said he'd do what he could."

"Without crossing Aunt Addy? That'll take talent."

Russell gestured in Matt's direction. "Hey, there she is!"

One look and Nita quickly placed her half-empty glass on a passing tray. Matt might be able to handle Cookie or Gloria alone, but the double whammy was ridiculous. "Give me the lobster," she said firmly, "and come on."

"Monterey is absolutely gorgeous at this time of year," Cookie was purring when they arrived. "I know you'd love it."

"But if you're staying in town," Gloria said with a smile as provocative as the bare midriff of her gown, "we'll probably run into each other at the club. I ride in the mornings. Between eight and ten."

"Since when?" Russell asked.

"Oh, Russie," she exclaimed with a flutter of lashes.

"You're always so busy with those old business deals. It serves you right if I invite someone else!"

Matt shook his head. "I don't ride. Where I come from, we canoe, fish, and play baseball."

"Baseball," Nita said approvingly. "Now *there's* a game."

"Well, the fishing is fantastic in Monterey," Cookie said. "We could hire a boat to go out into the bay and—"

"Cookie?" With a warning look Nita pressed a plate of lobster salad into her sister's unwilling hands. "And Gloria?" She passed the second plate to Gloria. "Russell fixed this just for you."

"Oh, Russie," Gloria squealed, "I wouldn't eat anything you fixed unless you tried it first."

Cookie's gaze wandered to a distant corner where the polo player and Aunt Addy were deep in conversation. Sugar was nowhere in sight. Her face brightened. "You know," she murmured, "Aunt Addy's the one who's really crazy about lobster salad."

"Tell her it's from me," Russell called after her as Gloria held a forkful to his mouth.

Nita pulled Matt away. "Bearing up?" she asked.

He felt his chest and tested his neck action. "Seem to be still intact. Is this typical?"

"More or less. Are you repulsed?"

"Let's say the evening's not my style."

"But that's not the worst, is it?"

"Call it perverse, silly, wasteful. . . . Shall I go on?"

"Chicago people," she said softly.

"I shouldn't criticize my future benefactors," he said with an ironic laugh.

"Don't kid yourself about the charity. My family might seem frivolous, but nobody gets anything for nothing from a Holiday."

"I'll keep that in mind."

Their eyes met. What she read in his didn't reassure her. "How about going outside for a minute? We have some unfinished business that has nothing to do with gold mines."

She laced her fingers through his, leading him past

the seats the musicians had temporarily abandoned and out into the darkness. She closed the French doors behind them. The raucous blend of laughter and voices faded.

Beneath the terrace, lights spangled the shoreline of the lake to the right and left, but the water's velvet blackness stretched before them in an endless expanse indistinguishable from the sky. A breeze carried the faint rhythm of waves cast against the shore and blew the floor-length pleated skirt of her dress into a swirling white fan. She turned her back on the view to study his set expression.

"Is this better?" she asked.

"Too bad we have to go back."

"We don't. Everyone has had time with you except me."

"It wasn't the arrangement I had in mind."

"No."

"You look like the proverbial million dollars tonight."

"Coming from you," she said, laughing, "I'm not sure how to take that."

"Make it five. Ten."

"Worth coming to see? In spite of everything?"

"You know you are."

He smoothed back tendrils of hair the wind had teased loose from her sleek chignon and cupped her face like a flower. A thin shaft of light from the apartment cast the strong planes of his face into deep relief. Slowly his hands traveled down her neck, around her shoulders. She felt their heat on her bare back, then the roughness of his coat as the fire in his eyes flared higher and he drew her close.

"Worth anything," he murmured.

His mouth caressed her hair as delicately as the wind. Slipping her arms inside his jacket, she pressed against him instinctively, feeling the hammering of his heart and echoing the strokes his hands were tracing on her skin.

"Matt, it's going to be all right."

"If everything depended on you and me, it might."

"No matter what."

"Nita—"

"Don't argue," she murmured. "This may not be the north woods, but it's dark and starlit and private. Doesn't that give you any ideas?"

"I should go inside before the ideas I have get out of control," he said, but his grip tightened. "I'm supposed to be wowing your relatives and making our fortune."

"Later."

Her mouth coquetted along the tendon of his neck and she felt his shuddering response through the length of their joined bodies. He groaned. "I promised one of your sisters I'd wait for her to come back. Your uncle wants a rematch, and your aunt has some mysterious assignment in mind for me later."

"Don't do it."

"Which?"

"Any of it."

"I thought I was a big success."

"That's the problem." Her lips brushed his jaw where the three moles were barely discernible, and she touched each of them delicately with the tip of her tongue. Inside the apartment music started up again.

"You're so successful it's dangerous," she said. "Half the women in that room would back you if you wanted to start digging under the Wrigley Building. If you leave here without the twins hanging around your neck, it will be a miracle. And Russell's probably courting brain fever trying to figure out how to get Gloria away from you without disabling her permanently."

"Tell them I'm spoken for," he said thickly.

"How about you telling me?"

"Nita . . ."

Her name faded into a moan as his mouth took possession of hers. Their lips blended, as she had known they would, with an intensity that swept away every sensation but the sweet passage from yearning toward release. His exploration lingered, yet its length could merely sketch the margins of their journey. The goal lay as potent and unplumbed as the massive body of water below.

The French doors swung open, and music crashed

over them along with a sudden wash of light. Their
kiss outlasted the dazzle for an instant before Matt
raised his head with a strangled exclamation. He thrust
her into the shelter of darkness, then released her and
turned to face the doors.

"There you are." Uncle Bo hailed them from the thresh-
old. "Been hunting you for twenty minutes, young
fellow."

"We . . . came out for some air, Uncle Bo," Nita said,
stepping forward.

"Is that what you call it?" He snorted, putting a
protective arm around her shoulders. "You've found a
tactician this time, Ni. Won't catch him napping."

"I know."

"Fine match, son."

"Thank you, sir."

"Give you double you won't beat me again."

Nita's eyes widened. Even in the half-light, Uncle
Bo's color looked abnormally high. Had winning really
made a better impression on him than losing? She
wasn't sure. If it had, she hoped Matt would have the
sense to quit while he was ahead.

"Time enough for these romantic shenanigans later,"
Uncle Bo continued. "A man has to court a woman
when he's covered with glory. Am I right, son? Shows
her he's worth the trouble."

"This is a party, Uncle Bo," Nita protested.

"Let 'em watch. Might teach some of 'em a thing or
two."

"I'll have to accept your offer, sir."

Uncle Bo chuckled. "Hate to take your money."

"Maybe it won't be necessary," Matt said with a smile.

Because Nita didn't trust herself to watch them play,
she learned the result of the game only when she overheard the twins' heated discussion as the last of the
guests drifted down the hall toward the elevators.

"How *could* Matt have beaten Uncle Bo?" Cookie
exclaimed.

"I saw him," Sugar said stubbornly. "I watched the
whole game. Afterward he even showed me how he
holds his cue."

She demonstrated with outstretched hands. Evidently Nita wasn't the only one who could imagine with graphic clarity the embrace required for such instruction. "He didn't!" Cookie wailed.

"If you hadn't been talking polo ponies with Peter and Aunt Addy," Sugar said, "he would have showed you too."

"I don't think Matt's right for Nita," Cookie confided as they walked down the hall toward their room.

"He's probably nothing but a phase."

"I invited him to Monterey."

"You didn't! So did I!"

As their door closed behind them Cookie's voice rose eagerly. "What did he say?"

Nita would have asked Matt the same question if she knew where he had gone. With a weary smile of farewell she shut the apartment door for the last time, then wandered aimlessly around the empty living room, turning out lights. Typical of everyone in the family to disappear, she thought, hoping Russell, not Matt, was seeing Gloria home.

In her room she exchanged Grecian pleats for a smoke-gray negligee. Bedroom doors opened and closed, followed by silence. Then her head lifted. Frozen in place, she heard the nearly soundless approach of footsteps she'd already learned to recognize. When a light tap sounded on her door, she sprang to answer it without a thought for her state of undress. The crystal knob came off in her hand.

"Damn!" she said under her breath. Was this Russell's own idea or had Aunt Addy coached? Effectively imprisoned, she whispered, "Matt? Is that you? I can't open my door."

"Please, Nita. I have to talk to you."

"I meant you have to open it from your side. The knob's come off. Russell must have had a busy evening. You'd better check your shower head before you use it. He gets indelible ink made up in special gelatine packets." She was laughing, but when the door swung open, Matt's expression sobered her instantly.

"What's wrong?"

"How fast can you get dressed?"

"An ex-model? About sixty seconds. Why?"

He held out two fifty-dollar bills. "There's a plane leaving for Houghton in forty-five minutes. What I won from your uncle would pay your fare."

Four

Nita's eyes widened. "What are you talking about?"

"We're too high off the ground for me to set up a ladder underneath your window," Matt said.

"You mean elope? You're joking!" She swallowed hard. "Aren't you?"

"No."

"Then you're right. We have to talk about this." In one decisive movement she put the doorknob on an ormolu chest, grabbed her negligee, and pulled him away from the door. "Not that I'm refusing automatically, you understand, but can you tell me what's going on?"

"I'm lucky you'll even listen," he said with a strangled laugh. He turned to the windows and thrust the ruched taffeta curtain aside. With his forehead propped on one clenched fist, he stared down at the traffic still streaming through the maze of city lights. "This wasn't the way I planned to ask you, but I doubt your family will let me get close enough for a second chance. Your sisters are tailing me like private eyes, your aunt's pegged me as a fortune hunter, and your uncle's decided only a pool hustler could outmaneuver him twice in a row."

"But they're wrong. You'll prove that tomorrow."

"They may be wrong about the specifics—" Lifting his head, he fixed his gaze on her face. "But don't kid yourself, Nita. They're right to be suspicious as hell. I don't belong here. I never will. And I want things from them I can't name or explain." He ran one hand through his dark hair. "When you phoned me that morning, I told myself coming to Chicago would be no different from trying to sell my idea to any other group of investors. The stakes might be higher, but the principle was the same. I thought I could sell an idea, but I was a fool not to realize selling out would be part of the deal."

"What do you mean?"

"I've been a lot of things—dirt poor, radical, hostile. But until now I've never been a fraud."

"You aren't!" she cried. "You didn't let Aunt Addy manipulate you. You didn't throw the billiard game to please Uncle Bo. Anyway, you can't count the party. Tonight should never have happened."

"It was bound to happen. That's what I'm trying to tell you. I should have expected your aunt and uncle to react the way they have. I'm an interloper angling for an entrée into a world I've always claimed to despise. What I'm doing doesn't make any sense even to *me* except as proof that somehow falling in love with you has turned my whole life upside down."

The pain in his eyes forced her to look away. "I'm sorry."

"Don't say that!" With a fierce gesture, he caught her by the shoulders. "I know I haven't any right to unload my problems on you like this. If I could offer you what you deserve, I wouldn't be standing here desperately trying to justify asking you to run away with me, but dammit, Nita, I can't help it. I have to go forward because I can't go back."

"Why isn't that the answer?"

He groaned. "Nothing's that simple. If feelings were enough to create a future for two people, I'd take my chances. I'd throw a blanket around you and carry you off, knowing somehow I'd find a way to make you happy. But I can't lie to myself, Nita. This is the real world and feelings aren't enough. No amount of wanting you will change that."

She tried to muster a smile. "Being carried off sounds pretty romantic."

No answering glint of humor lit his eyes. "What I'm talking about doesn't register with you at all, does it?

You can't see how everything in this room, this apartment, your past, your lifestyle, stands in the way of our being able to build a life together."

"I hear what you're saying, Matt," she exclaimed impatiently. "But we're living in the twentieth century. Nobody expects to spend their whole lives surrounded by people like themselves. We move all over the country. We change lifestyles the way we change clothes. People aren't looking for partners who went to the same school, the same church, and mirror their own experiences down to the last detail."

"You and I could be different breeds."

"That's not fair! You're talking about my family, not me."

"I'm talking about reality. I love you, but that doesn't change our situation. How much do you really know about me, Nita?"

She avoided his eye. "Less than you know about me."

"Almost nothing."

"I don't care! It doesn't matter!"

"Yes," he said quietly. "It does."

"If you felt that way," she burst out, "you should have refused my offer the morning I made it. Didn't you understand that the more time we spent together, the more I'd care? Why let me go on hoping if you knew in advance nothing could work out? I never pretended to be any different than I am. I told you what my family was like."

"Nita, don't—" Relaxing the grip he'd clamped on her arms, he folded her close. "Can't you guess why I had to come?" he murmured into her hair.

"None of this makes sense to me."

He fingered the lace edging on the yoke of her robe. "I couldn't stay away," he said at last. "I came for the same reason I want to lose when we argue and I take you in my arms, even though I know each time I do will make it harder to let you go. I can't help myself. When you smile I lose track of everything except the color of your eyes and the way your face lights up. I couldn't begin to explain why a casual gesture of yours takes my breath away and leaves me shaking, but it does."

"Does that mean I should pack?"

"I don't want to hurt you."

Her grasp around him tightened. "That can only happen if you shut me out."

"Nita, I—"

"No, Matt, listen. If you can't trust me for any other reason, at least trust what I say about my own feelings. In spite of all the differences you see between us, we want the same thing—a chance to be together without regrets. But the only way we'll have that is to keep everything up front and clear. You can make your presentation tomorrow, exactly the way you intended. No facades. No images. My family doesn't kid around with topics as serious as making money. If a full-blooded Indian walked down off the reservation with a great prospect, none of them would turn it down because his ancestors hadn't come over on the *Mayflower*, or he wasn't wearing a Brooks Brothers suit, or his only backer was an unemployed blonde."

"The description's close."

"Then will you talk to them tomorrow? If you won't do it for me—for us—at least you owe it to the mine to try. If there is a mine."

"What do you mean, *if* there is a mine!"

"Just checking." She managed a tiny smile. "I'd never hear the last of it if I brought in a scam."

"Will being in love with my partner count against me?"

"It might not be a selling point with the twins."

His chuckle rumbled beneath her ear. "I'll make an effort not to be too obvious."

"Not in public."

His embrace tightened around her for an instant. "Don't tempt me. All I need is to have your aunt catch me leaving your room at three A.M. She'd mistrust my intentions if I tried to *give* her a gold mine."

Nita sighed. Preventive suspicion was Aunt Addy's strong point. Nevertheless, when her aunt appeared in the hall while Matt was helping refasten the knob to Nita's door a few minutes later, their self-denial seemed a cruel waste.

"I hope Nita reminded you breakfast is at nine, Matthew?" Aunt Addy said, raising her brows with purely illusory mildness. Although Matt managed to look as suave as any man could when discovered kneeling beside a seductively clad woman in the early hours of the morning, he colored faintly under his tan.

"Matt was helping fix my door, Aunt Addy."

"On the spot with trusty pocketknife in hand," her aunt murmured. "What enviable resource."

"Wilderness survival tactics, ma'am. See you at nine."

Aunt Addy watched the door to his room close behind him before she turned back to Nita. "I expect Russell to form these unfortunate attachments, dear. In his own way, your brother's quite naive. But I never dreamed I'd have to worry about you too."

"Me?"

"Of course Gloria lacks Matthew's finesse."

Nita stared at her. "You're comparing Matt to Gloria?"

"Don't raise your voice, dear."

"You don't know him!"

"I paid special attention this evening. I found him far more interesting than the twins' polo player, who is a rather inferior conversationalist, although I'm told he has a marvelous seat."

"Matt's a talented man, Aunt Addy."

"I'm sure he is," her aunt said sweetly, "which makes me quite curious to hear the real purpose of his visit. I suppose we'll have a chance to discover more tomorrow?"

Nita swallowed hard. "We've been talking about . . . about forming a partnership."

"In what, dear?"

"Gold," she said unhappily.

"Gold?" Her aunt's eyes lit with a dangerous gleam. "Well, then, I see I'm not far off, after all."

Sleep didn't come easily to Nita after that conversation, and she entered the dining room well before the appointed hour. Janie, the maid, was watching Matt butter his toast as though it were the most captivating activity she'd witnessed in months. Sliding into a chair opposite him, Nita caught a glitter of amusement in his eyes.

"Janie was just telling me the polo player left early," he said.

"A prudent man," Nita murmured.

"Or a coward." Matt raised his glass of orange juice to her in a toast. "Luckily some of us are made of sterner stuff."

The twins burst into the room like bubbles and gravitated to both sides of Matt with cries of greeting. Their flyaway hairstyles and brilliantly striped blouses cut low around knobby necklaces made them look more like rock singers than market analysts. Russell followed, rubbing his hands together in unfeigned good cheer.

"Well, folks," he announced, "I finally did it."

"Don't ask him what," Cookie said.

"As if that ever stopped him," her twin added.

"I filled Gloria's hair dryer with charcoal dust. I just wish I could be there to see her face when she uses it this morning."

Taking his place at the head of the table, Uncle Bo shook his head, either at his nephew's action or at the bowl of oatmeal awaiting him. " 'Fraid you've gone over the line this time, my boy."

"What do you mean? It's a great gag."

"Russell," Cookie said, "when are you going to learn that normal women don't like whoopie cushions hidden under their seats?"

"Or gunpowder sprinkled in their pants cuffs—"

"So you can touch matches to them?"

"Hey, I'd forgotten that one." Russell chortled in happy reminiscence. "Cuffs disappeared like magic!"

Uncle Bo, who had been toying with his oatmeal during this exchange, glanced at his watch, cleared his throat, and leaned toward Matt. "When I'm off-color, Ad makes me eat the same pap my mother fed me as a boy. I grew up in Hibbing, Minnesota, son, where we had winters cold enough to shrivel a fellow's insides if they weren't full. Fine mining country around there, though."

"That's right, sir."

Nita could have kissed her uncle for introducing the topic of mining so spontaneously, but when her aunt appeared on the stroke of nine, she remembered collusion was one of Aunt Addy's favorite tactics. Uncle Bo must have been given instructions to check Matt's information.

"Sleep well, everyone?" her aunt asked.

Her gaze rested on Matt as if by chance, the surest sign her skepticism hadn't lessened. Crossing her fingers and praying she wasn't leading him into a trap, Nita said brightly, "You and Matt ought to compare notes, Uncle Bo."

"Ever been up that way, son?"

To Nita's relief, Matt smiled. "Couldn't miss it. Mining engineers dream about sites like the Mesabi Range. It's a classic example of the kind of simple geological structure that makes a great mining district—a rich ore lode with the potential for cheap development and extraction."

"Well, I guess you appreciate the technical side more than I did," Uncle Bo said, straightening and looking more interested. He never liked his wife's victories to come too easily. "I was always more eager to be on the water than underground myself. That's why I chose to go to sea. You wouldn't think a man would run into much mining on shipboard, but one time I had an opportunity to watch Chinese girls prospecting for jade. Used to wade up and down the rivers. Girls are Yin, you see, and jade is Yang, so there was an attraction between the two. All they had to do was pick up the pieces when they touched their feet. Of course, they were naked as jaybirds."

Russell chuckled. "No wonder you watched!"

"Russell, dear, your uncle simply intended to point out the role superstition plays in the search for easy wealth. But I suppose to men in your calling"—Aunt Addy smiled at Matt as graciously as though she entertained suspected con artists at every meal—"any method may prove useful. My father made a great deal of money in oil. I actually visited a number of wells with him as a girl because he made it a rule never to become involved in anything he couldn't see, smell, touch, or taste. Perhaps from your point of view, basing an investment on tangible products seems old-fashioned?"

"Gold is pretty tangible," Nita said.

"Of course, dear, you *did* mention gold. I must have put it out of my mind. It's so difficult to imagine anyone less ravaged looking than Walter Huston or Humphrey Bogart tramping around in the heat with a beard and a burro."

"I'm afraid you are a little old-fashioned there, ma'am," Matt said. "Most prospecting these days is done by computer. I still spend summers in the field, but in Ontario a canoe is more useful than a burro."

Nita awarded the point to their side.

"I adore men with beards," Cookie murmured.

"Do you have some pet spot, son?"

Matt and Nita exchanged glances. The moment had come. She wiped her damp hands surreptitiously on her napkin and gave him a full-wattage smile of encouragement.

"As a matter of fact, sir," he began after a pause so long Nita had to wipe her hands again, "I'm ready to start taking final test samples on a site I've been studying for years. With enough backing I could bring in a minable claim for the biggest untouched gold lode on the continent by the end of the season."

Russell came alert with a jerk. "Where?"

"On the eastern shore of Lake Superior."

"Mineral rights clear?"

"One line of my projected site abuts Indian land, but the rest is available."

"What odds a claim will go to development?"

"About five percent in Ontario, but this is an exceptional situation. Usually Canadian gold is scattered out in narrow quartz veins. Here, there's a wide band of ore between volcanic and sedimentary rocks. It's one of those simple structures I was mentioning to your uncle."

"Sounds like a nice gamble."

Nite rejoiced at the speculative gleam in her brother's eyes. "That's right, Russell," she said. "The backers either end up with egg all over their faces or come in big against the odds. *Very* big."

"Yeah," he said thoughtfully.

Uncle Bo leaned forward. "What you might call a sporting chance of success, is that it?"

"Yes, sir. But I don't bet if I'm likely to lose." Matt grinned. "I guess you know that."

"I was off my game yesterday. Don't count on a repeat."

"I'm ready when you are."

Uncle Bo snorted, but his normal color had returned. "See, Ad? I told you the boy doesn't lack spunk."

Like a general whose troops are weakening, Aunt Addy retreated to higher ground. "Gold exercises such a powerful effect on people's imaginations it must be a temptation to see a single fragment, even a bit of dust the size of a pinhead, as evidence for a river of wealth." Her gaze lingered on Matt. "Or to assume others might be taken in by the same delusion."

Matt's look didn't waver. "This lode is no dream. As far back as 1665 Jesuits were shipping gold to France from the spot I have in mind. Two veins were discovered in the vicinity in 1869, but never mined, and interest fell away until maps made in 1931 suggested major deposits."

"Something went wrong?"

"On the contrary, quite a few prospectors took the hint. I've talked to some who would have pursued what they found if the price of gold had been what it is today."

The twins looked at each other. Quotations on the gold market must have streamed across their eyeballs, for the effect on them was electrifying.

"Why, next year," Cookie exclaimed, "we're predicting—"

"Another record rise in gold! Oh, Matt," Sugar breathed, "right from the beginning I knew our interests were compatible."

Cookie glared at her twin. "I could help put together some terrific statistics to impress potential backers. How many do you have so far?"

"One," Nita said quietly. "I'm backing him."

Silence fell over the table, accompanied by the turn of every head in Nita's direction. She tossed back her hair and smiled bravely at Matt, watching his gaze travel around the circle of faces. Mentally, she tallied the positions along with him: risk intrigued Russell almost as much as profit, so he'd probably be on their side; Uncle Bo and the twins might go either way; unfortunately, Aunt Addy's suspicions hadn't subsided an inch.

"I don't expect you to take my word," Matt said. "The documentation is in my pack."

He rose with an easy grace that brought a lump to Nita's throat as she watched him leave the room. Carrying that chip on his shoulder had trained his supple walk more effectively than carrying a book on her head had trained her as a model. In his stride she read the kind of consummate self-control under stress it had taken her years to learn—along with enough pride to drive him away from her for good if the family rejected his proposal.

Russell recovered first. "Gutsy guy, but a scheme that size is a hell of a risk."

"You're taking a big chance, Ni."

She managed to smile at her uncle. "How could I go wrong with a billiard champ?"

"I had no idea you'd committed yourself so deeply, dear," Aunt Addy said. "Surely modeling hasn't been lucrative enough for you to invest on that scale?"

"It's not, Aunt Addy. Matt needs your help."

"I've got it!" Russell's face shone. "Holiday Mines!"

"I'm not sure he wants—"

But her brother already had his pen out of his pocket with the top unscrewed. "A family syndicate! For the grubstake, percentages would be our best bet." He grabbed Nita's starched linen napkin and scribbled numbers on it. "We'd each subscribe for a certain number of units worth, say, a thousand dollars apiece, to be traded in for shares after the discovery. Have to make sure we control enough of the total so we'll get the name. How about it, Uncle Bo? Might have another coup here."

"If he's as handy with a surveyor's kit as he is with a cue, I'm game."

"I'll back him too," Sugar cried, jumping up from her chair. "Put me down for a share at least as big as Nita's."

"Bring my checkbook," Cookie called after her.

"What about you, Aunt Addy?" Russell asked. "Good for a couple of thou on a dark horse?"

"I do not bet on impulse," she said through pursed lips.

The document Matt laid on the table before her certainly wasn't frivolous reading. Russell snatched it to fan its hundred-plus pages until he came to those filled with figures. He whistled. "Not talking peanuts here."

"I believe he offered his report to me, dear," Aunt Addy said, "and I intend to read every word with great care. I'm especially interested in the part about the site adjoining Indian land. Coming from the Upper Peninsula, Matthew, I imagine you realize how Native American claims can cloud an issue?"

Matt's jaw tightened. "Indian rights always seemed pretty clear to me. They're not the interlopers on their land."

"Well," she said smoothly, "however you describe the problem, we wouldn't want anything of that kind involved here."

Nita stifled Matt's response with a warning hand on his arm. "Why don't you and I let the family talk things over?"

He gave her a thin smile. "I could use some air."

"Let's go see the mine at the Science Museum," Cookie said.

Sugar frowned. "But it's a *coal* mine."

"What difference does that make? It's so romantic riding those creaky little cars in the dark."

"You two can't leave before we thrash out a draft," Russell protested. "There's a lot of nitty-gritty involved here; big sums at stake. I'll have my legal staff take a peek too. They spent weeks working out the hotel deal."

"If it's a question of watching out for Matt's interests," Sugar said nobly, "I'll be happy to stay."

Cookie sulked. "We'll catch up with you later."

"Can I borrow your car, Russell?" Nita asked. Her eyes were dancing with mischief as she made a one-handed catch of the keys he lobbed to her. "And try to write a contract that doesn't blow up in Matt's face when he opens it, will you?"

"Hey, give me a break! Do I ever joke about money? Drop by the office in about an hour." Russell winked at them. "Maybe I can talk Aunt Addy round by then."

With a sidelong glance at her silent companion, Nita put the car key in the ignition. "You look terribly glum for a man about to land a fortune. I thought we'd celebrate."

"It can't be this easy."

"If Aunt Addy finds any loopholes in that report, she'll give you a run for your money. I warned you she was sharp."

"When she came up with the bit about Indian rights, I almost blew the whole thing."

"Needling people is one of her specialties."

"She sure struck a raw nerve. Look, Nita, there's something I—"

Shaking her head, she laid a finger on his mouth. "Not another word. I refuse to hear any high-minded reasons why this can never work out and why the two of us haven't a chance of being happy until the whole world changes." Shutting off the ignition. she swiveled around to face him. "Why can't you simply admit to being terrific in there just now? You had everybody in the palm of your hand."

"Except your aunt."

"Come on, Matt, what do you expect? Her pride is tied up in her judgments. They count for her as much as—as keeping your word counts for you."

"But that's what I'm trying to tell you—"

"Look, are you conning us, or is your report solid?"

"It's solid."

"Then will you stop worrying? Aunt Addy reads financial statements the way I read romances. We're natural skeptics hoping to become believers. Once she gets into the facts and figures, she'll forget her conviction that no attractive man can be up to any good and start visualizing the potential. Then we won't have to think about winning her approval as much as how to keep her from taking over a controlling interest."

"You thought the mine was a scam and I had a lot more rapport with you than I have with your aunt."

"Because you flung the idea at me out of the blue!"

"That was a reason?"

"It was natural. I have an ego, too, you know. With my own share of doubts." She bent her head, the memory of Aunt Addy's suspicions making her more vulnerable than she wanted to be. "When you seemed more interested in spending my money than in spending time with me, can you blame me for being afraid it wasn't me you wanted?"

"We've never *had* any time to spend together. We're due at your brother's office in less than an hour and we don't even have a place to go that's more private than a No Parking zone. Nita . . ." His voice softened as he pushed back the curtain of hair that hid her face from him. "Look at me. Whatever you come to believe about me—if I fail you out of clumsiness or in any other way—it won't be, it could never be, because I don't want you."

"When Aunt Addy doubted you," she muttered, "you handed her a hundred pages of proof instead of a hard time."

Laughing, he bent toward her. "If you want proof, I'd rather use another format for the documentation. What do you think about this for a title?"

He brushed her mouth lingeringly with his lips. As an opener it claimed her complete attention. Worse titles appeared on the best-seller list every week.

"It's a topic that interests me," she said.

He laughed. "More than mining?"

"It has more universal appeal."

"I'm still doing drafts. The style may need polishing."

Settling back with closed eyes, she said, "It's content that counts."

Not that she had any objections to his style. None at all. His sense of pacing was acute, his choice of detail subtle. To judge by its length and depth, the kiss seemed equal to articulating a complex development of ideas in a vocabulary that was nothing if not varied and original. There were even a few unfamiliar terms whose significance she wanted to explore more completely later. In fact, he went a long way toward expanding the whole language of kissing, if not the genre. Nevertheless, she'd been right to emphasize content. Content was his real strength.

When he came up for air, she murmured, "I hope I don't have to wait too long for the sequel."

"I have plenty of material."

"Too bad about all these distractions."

"You mean like teaching and prospecting for gold?"

"Mmm."

"You'll have to join me in the woods."

She smiled. "Camping?"

"The Canadian prospecting season opens in May."

"Good."

Nestled deep in his arms, her spirit too satisfied for her to attend to a crick developing in her back, she watched the twins emerge from the condominium in a tearing hurry, flag a taxi, and vanish in the direction of the Museum of Science and Industry. Two thousand exhibits (and who knew how many romantic patrons and blue-uniformed guards) awaited them once they convinced themselves they'd missed their quarry in the coal mine. A little later Russell followed, looking as intent as though he were hot on the trail of a deal that would trump Donald Trump.

"Aunt Addy must have weakened," Nita murmured contentedly.

They celebrated this possibility at length, but eventually, driven to acknowledge that kissing in bucket seats, like modeling, was an activity best suited to contortionists, she shifted in his arms. When she opened her eyes, her new angle presented the fatal earlobe in irresistible proximity. Never sympathetic to his theory of postponing gratification, she gathered it delicately into her mouth.

He shuddered and drew her closer. "Careful there. We'll be arrested for more than parking."

"I couldn't help it. I don't have your control."

"Mine is eroding faster than a dust bowl. When your uncle asked if I was prospecting in one particular spot and you smiled at me, my mind went blank. All I could think of were excuses to leave the table, take you back to my room, and lock the door behind us for the rest of the day. My concentration didn't go back to normal for about five minutes."

"Were those kisses a sample of what I missed?"

"More or less," he said with a grin. "I was a little hampered by the steering wheel."

"You want to know the most convincing part of the proof?"

"The length of time I can hold my breath?"

"No," she said, laughing as she sat up to start the car, "the fact that we're fifteen minutes late for our meeting with Russell and you never once checked your watch."

They entered her brother's carpeted office, with its million-dollar view of the tinted-glass towers of South Wacker Drive, to find Russell totally absorbed in a phone conversation.

"What happened to your sense of humor, Gloria?" he shouted into the mouthpiece as he rattled the plunger furiously with a finger. Blank amazement covered his face as he slammed down the receiver and looked at them. "She hung up on me!"

"Ever thought of changing your style?" Nita asked.

"Wait until she hears about this new deal," he grumbled. "She'll be begging me to take her back."

The new deal could mean only one thing. Nita's spirits soared. "Or else she'll start shipping Matt booby-trapped supplies," she said gaily.

"Stuff like imitation cans of beans?"

"Nita, for Pete's sake," Matt said. "Don't give him any ideas."

A grin flitted across Russell's face, but as he flipped

open the single folder centered on his desk, which was the size of Uncle Bo's billiard table, and folded his hands importantly over the material it contained, his expression changed to one of weighty solemnity. The single sheet of paper in the folder could never hold enough details for a long-term agreement, Nita thought. With apprehension as sudden as her burst of high spirits, she reached for Matt's hand.

"Aunt Addy didn't . . ." She choked on the possibility that a catastrophe had been brewing in secret and snagged a fresh breath. ". . . didn't come around?"

"Have to be realistic. These sums are not small potatoes."

"She doesn't believe the lode exists," Matt said quietly.

"I wouldn't put it that way. Under pressure she might admit you've written a hell of a convincing proposal. Seemed sort of surprised when she finished looking it over, in fact."

"Then it's me she doesn't trust."

Russell looked uncomfortable. "In a word, yes."

"And the rest of you agreed with her?" Nita's color rose as she glared at him. "Uncle Bo didn't say anything? Or the twins?"

"You know how Aunt Addy is when she gets worked up."

"Oh, damn!"

Matt's grin was painful. "How long before she has me run out of town?"

"Wait a minute. It's not that bad. Would I have waited for you if I didn't have a counteroffer? You were so late I thought maybe the twins had caught up with you and blown my scoop." Russell shot his wrist out of his coat sleeve and punched a button to activate the display on his watch. The motion simultaneously set off a chime rendition of "For He's a Jolly Good Fellow," slid open doors concealing a bar at the end of the room, and triggered a fall of ice cubes into the serving container of its refrigerator. "Cute, huh? You can get the damnedest gadgets nowadays. Drink, anyone?"

"Russell! Quit playing games!" Nita cried. "What's the offer?"

"Calm down and I'll tell you. Knowing how tight you two are—I mean, you didn't need to hit me over the head with a club the other night when I—"

"Russell, the offer," Nita said warningly.

"Okay, okay. I just wanted you to know I did the best I could for you. I really think this will be a honey of a deal, but negotiating with Aunt Addy is tougher than handling the whole bunch down at city hall. If they had her protecting the city's interests, I'd be out four hundred and fifty thousand dollars in taxes yearly, or more than—"

"Russell!"

"Right. The offer. Don't snap my head off. Uncle Bo and the twins are behind this one hundred percent. We're only talking about the exploratory phase and, of course, it's contingent on the family retaining rights for first negotiation on all claims, if and when filed."

Nita looked over at Matt, whose eyes burned in a face of stony rigidity. Would he bend for her sake? she wondered. How much? A bleak chill settled in the vicinity of her heart. So far, he hadn't shown much inclination to bend at all.

"We're ready to supply fifty-five percent of the development costs—a controlling interest, see? That was my idea." Russell warmed to his task as he went along. "So we hang onto the possibility of calling the whole shebang Holiday Mines. The deal boils down to this: If you two can raise the other forty-five percent in thirty days, you're in business."

"Thirty days?" Nita exclaimed. "That's impossible!"

"Tricky, maybe, but not *impossible*." Russell paused long enough to look from her flushed face to Matt's grim one and to shrug in sympathy. "Well, I did the best I could. According to Aunt Addy, a setup like this is the ultimate test of character."

Five

Nita followed Matt over to the long windows where the pungent, honking vitality of the city was spread beneath them. Despite twenty stories' distance and a wall of glass, its streets seemed more accessible than the thoughts of the man beside her. She longed to touch his arm, say his name, do anything, in fact, to draw him away from his dark deliberations. But the clamped angle of his jaw stopped her. After her family's cynical offer, what right had she to plead?

Russell lacked her inhibitions. He cleared his throat. "Actually, there are a couple of other conditions."

Matt turned. A dangerous glitter lit his eye. "What are they? Am I supposed to wear a little bell to announce I'm a social leper? Do you want to implant a tracking device so I can't run off with the funds? Or would your aunt be satisfied if I simply punched a time clock set up on some handy rock?"

"Is he kidding?" Russell asked Nita.

"Not . . . exactly," she said in a strangled voice.

"Well, look here, Lamartine, I have a sense of humor, but money's no joking matter. Anybody'd think we hadn't been perfectly square with you."

Her brother's air of injured dignity brought the faintest hint of a smile to Matt's mouth, and her hand flew to her throat to suppress a gasp of hope. If Matt hung onto his sense of humor, there was a chance that someday they could laugh about the whole affair together. All the way to the bank. Maybe all the way to a justice of the peace.

"Want to hear the conditions or not?" Russell asked huffily.

"Shoot."

"What we're proposing is nothing out of the ordinary. Nothing unreasonable. You can ask anybody. We want to establish two simple measures, as much for your protection as for our—"

"Russell," Nita said, "you're protesting too much."

"Let me handle this, will you? And let the man make up his own mind? Backers for a long shot with nothing to show but paper don't grow on trees. He knows what he's up against with a project like this. Or if he doesn't, he damn well ought to. All we want are minimal safeguards while he's trying to get the rest of the money and the claims are being staked." Russell turned to Matt and shook his head. "You can see why women don't belong in the negotiating process. They're always getting sidetracked by some subjective issue."

This time Matt did grin as he placed his hand on Nita's arm to hold back her outraged response. "Let's hear the conditions."

"As I said, they're completely straightforward. First of all, Nita represents the family's interests and in that capacity she countersigns—"

"Oh, no!"

Her brother scowled in her direction. "She countersigns all checks."

"That's insulting!" she cried.

But Matt's grip tightened on her arm. "The purpose is clear enough. What's the second?"

"All expenditures for supplies and all supply orders go through my office."

Nita groaned. These were minimal safeguards? Not content with driving a wedge into all her dealings with Matt, harassing him at every turn, and reminding him constantly of the family's mistrust, Aunt Addy evidently intended to sabotage the whole project. Nobody in his right mind would let Russell within a hundred miles of his supplies.

"Tied my hands pretty thoroughly, didn't you?"

Russell coughed modestly. "We tried to cover the basic contingencies."

"And you knew I had no choice."

"Could have been worse. The twins wanted to countersign."

To Nita's astonishment, Matt laughed. "I guess I owe you something for sparing me that. Where do I sign?"

"Right on the dotted line. But don't use the pen in the desk set. It squirts out the top when you press down. Gets a laugh every time, but my secretary swears if she has to retype one more ink-splattered contract, she'll quit."

"I could sign in blood."

"Save it until we're dividing up the claims." As Russell slid the contract over the polished mahogany, he grinned triumphantly and poked Nita with his elbow. "How about that? Do I deal, or do I deal? Aunt Addy bet he wouldn't come around, but I figured there was a seventy-thirty chance. Is she going to burn when I tell her she owes me a week in the Bahamas for two."

Watching Matt sign his name gave Nita a moment of pure, unadulterated delight. The family had done its worst, but instead of a disaster, the result would be hours, days, and weeks of time she and Matt might spend together. Under those circumstances, the task of matching the family's share of the funding would be a treat, a golden opportunity in every sense of the word. She gave him a radiant smile as he straightened up. "How soon do we start?" she asked.

"I'll start on Thursday. The Prospectors and Developers Association is meeting in Toronto. It's the one time of the year prospectors hobnob with stock promoters and mining company executives."

"What do you mean, *you'll* start? I'll go with you."

The expression that crossed Matt's face would have made a fortune for an artist who could capture it for the cover of a romance. Nita couldn't mistake how much he wanted her along. Her color rose. Was he about to sweep her into his arms, carry her off for days and nights of passion, and put their relationship on the highroad to page one hundred and eighty-two at last?

She stepped toward him, but instead of reaching for her, he ran one hand through his dark hair as though trying to brush away an impulse he couldn't handle. "Not this time, Nita. I'm the one your aunt wants to test. I have to handle this phase alone."

"But you can't—"

"Maybe not," he interrupted with a wry smile. "All the same, I intend to have a damn good try."

"That wasn't what I was going to say! I meant you can't leave me behind."

"Only physically."

Only? She opened her mouth to protest, but the look in his eyes made her swallow hard. "Why is it," she muttered, "every time you start acting heroic, I end up deprived?"

Russell cleared his throat again. "Let's cut the soul-searching for a minute and get back to business. Toronto sounds like a smart place to start. Holiday's a good name there. Mention Uncle Bo."

"Not unless all else fails."

"I could mention him," Nita said. "I'm not shy."

"You won't be there."

"I thought we were partners. Aren't we in this together?"

"I just signed an agreement that says we're in together for fifty-five percent. For the other forty-five, I'm on my own."

"That wasn't what I wanted."

"Collecting aspersions on my character wasn't my original goal either," he said, "but it seems I have a choice between turning my other cheek or decamping in disgrace. Your aunt thinks greed is my motive. You know why I have to prove she's wrong."

"I do! And I want to help!"

"Then don't tempt me to take you along. Nothing I want for us can happen unless this project works. That means no distractions. And it means making your family understand that when I agreed to let you sign the checks, I wasn't agreeing to let them call the shots."

Russell frowned. "Now wait a minute here. Nita has every right to go."

"Wasn't the test for me to put this together on my own?"

"I get your drift, Lamartine. Thumb to the nose at the family, point of honor, and all that. But why risk the whole deal for a gesture? If you deliver, Aunt Addy will change her tune soon enough. And a woman usually comes in handy at an affair like this—greasing the social wheels, laughing in the right places, chatting up the wives. Taking Nita along makes perfect sense."

"Not a diabolical twist in the character test?"

"She's supposed to represent the family's interests. It's in the contract!"

"Fine. But sending her to Toronto is a contingency you forgot to write in." Matt flung open the office door, then paused. "And tell your aunt that if I can turn down a bigger temptation than the combined Holiday fortune, the rest of her test will be a snap."

Russell stared after Matt's disappearing back. "Is he kidding again?"

"No." She was thinking hard. "He's not."

"Aunt Addy may be way off base about him, but he's pretty damned independent. Better keep an eye on him."

"Save your breath, Russell. You don't understand him."

"All the same, if I were you, I'd go to Toronto."

She grinned as she hoisted her heavy shoulder bag. "Russell, I'm way ahead of you."

Because plane service was better from Chicago than from Houghton, Nita arrived at Toronto's Royal York Hotel way before Matt and had plenty of time to check into the suite she had booked for Lamartine-Holiday Development, cancel his reservation for a single room, and register for the convention. She also had time to worry about how Matt would react. In order to keep the two halves of their infant partnership on speaking terms, she decided their first meeting had better take place in public. Business before pleasure.

The bellhop, entranced by the quantity of luggage he had carried to her room and the consequent size of his tip, agreed to inform Mr. Lamartine that his partner would be waiting on the convention floor. From the goggle-eyed reaction of the representative of the Prospectors and Developers Association who'd accepted her registration, and her glimpse of a meeting, which resembled a crowded stag session, she figured Matt would have no difficulty finding her.

Before she set out to test the reaction of a couple of thousand men to the latest look in prospectors, Nita surveyed the suite's sitting room, envisioning her daring choice of accommodations as a setting for the weekend to come. Instinct warned her that the best project in the world couldn't be promoted from a hole-in-the-wall—not even the Royal York's version of a hole—but the management had created a satisfying ambiance which would do for both purposes of her trip.

The circular dining table could adapt to candlelight and privacy as well as to chic cocktail parties for prospective backers. Two decorous bedrooms opened off a single luxurious bath. The decor murmured of creature comforts, stability, and enough money in the bank to squander some of it on hospitality. All the room needed was a personal touch men would remember without noticing, and women would both notice and appreciate. Fresh flowers. When she closed the suite door behind her, she'd already decided to order some tomorrow. After Matt calmed down.

The convention floor was filled with exhibits of every size and description—snowshoes and backpacks for the well-outfitted prospector, software for developers, geophysical measuring devices, and pneumatic drills. As she wound her way past them, heads turned like falling dominoes. For an ex-model, making sure the Lamartine-Holiday tag pinned to the front of her dress was easily readable presented no more of a problem than summoning an easy smile, and the number of people who paused to jot down the name gratified her. She was making progress in her first half-hour.

Bypassing a room given over to speeches on topics

like "Applications of Lithogeochemistry to Tin Exploration," she concentrated on building an information base from which to converse with backers. Matt found her poring over displays offered by small joint-venture companies like Golden Sceptre and Goliath Gold Mines.

"What the hell are you doing here?" he said under his breath.

"Is that all the welcome I get?"

"Weren't you listening when I said I had to come alone?"

She'd anticipated a certain amount of initial exasperation, but instead of offering one of the soothing replies she'd prepared, she found herself admiring the fresh brilliance anger lent his dark eyes. "I missed you," she murmured.

"The phone company is supposed to take care of that."

"Some things don't travel over the wires."

His jaw tightened. "This is a business trip, Nita."

"I came on business."

"Very funny."

"Aren't you glad to see me? Personally?"

"Glad? I wouldn't be normal if I didn't admit you're a major threat to my peace of mind."

"I've been attracting attention."

"That's obvious," he said, scowling at patrons of nearby booths who were showing exaggerated interest in diamond drill bits and longitudinal projection charts. "This conversation couldn't have more eavesdroppers if I were giving the exact location of the lode."

"By afternoon Lamartine-Holiday will be on everyone's lips."

He groaned and dragged her aside. "We have to talk."

"Your place or mine?"

"The lobby will do. I know better than to try to argue with you in private. Anyway, the people at the desk screwed up my room reservation. I'm still waiting for them to figure out what happened to my single . . ." His eyes narrowed and the angle of his jaw stood out as he said, "You're behind that, too, aren't you?"

"Mmm." She expanded her admiration to include the

flare of irritation sculpting his nostrils and smiled up at him. "Giving in gracefully is your only option."

"You think so?"

He hustled her past knots of conventioneers toward the reservations counter. She relaxed into his grip. Being with him was half the battle, and even misplaced passion could lead to better things. Once he worked through his frustration, she'd explain the advantages of having a suite. If he remained unconvinced, she could demonstrate a few.

"There's no point in pestering the desk clerks," she said. "They're booked solid. In fact, while I was checking in, one of them gave your room away to a bearded fellow in a plaid flannel shirt who looked as though he had his burro parked outside."

"Damn!"

"A high proportion of prospectors must be bachelors."

"Only promoters can afford to marry," he said grimly.

"For a minute I wondered if there'd be any wives for me to chat up."

"The problem's academic. I'm putting you on the next plane."

"No, you're not."

Her mouth was set with determination equal to his. Nothing short of dynamite or the complete collapse of their relationship was going to move her from the Royal York.

"This is my operation, Nita."

"Okay, I won't argue about that, but I'm not leaving, either. We started out as partners. I didn't set any conditions then, and nothing my family's done has changed the way I feel."

"That's why you're watching every step I take?"

"You're an engineer. What you know and do is the heart of the whole project. Just because no one else could approach my family doesn't mean I want you to turn into a salesman! From the beginning I expected the business end to be my responsibility. Give me a chance, Matt. Whether you admit it or not, raising this much money will take all the guts, energy, and savvy we both can muster. Can't you trust me to hold up my end? I've trusted you."

"That's not the point."

"Originally it was the *whole* point!"

Before he could answer, a meaty hand fell on his shoulder. "Hey, there, Matt! Still trying to put the touch on someone for that crazy scheme of yours?"

"My position's improved a bit. How've you been?"

The stranger's guffaw revealed an abundance of gold-filled molars. "Vancouver suits me. Real sporting investors out west."

"Are you putting in money or taking it out?" Nita asked with a smile.

"Both."

She gave Matt a quick glance. If the stranger was a possible backer, some sign would give the fact away. She wasn't deterred when it came in the form of an unpartnerlike glare. "Going to introduce me?" she said sweetly.

"Nita Holiday. Pez McKinnon."

A callused palm engulfed hers and a pair of gray eyes took in her name tag. "Lamartine-Holiday, eh? If this young lady's your new partner, boy, I'd say you were riding a crest."

"Matt will be filing claims this summer."

Pez looked surprised. "That so?"

"I've some new maps I think will interest you," Matt said.

"They might. They might indeed. Have to wait till I get the wife settled in, though. Mining talk bores her stiff until it translates into fancy china and fur coats."

Nita smiled at him. "I can sympathize."

"You offering to take her off my hands?"

"Matt's going to be busy once the news gets out," she said, meeting his sharp look with unwavering poise. "I wouldn't want you to miss your chance to talk."

Pez's laugh rolled out again as he motioned to a stocky, well-girdled woman standing beside a set of luggage completely covered with logos. "Come on over here, Audrey. Someone I want you to meet. Looks like Matt's found himself a real sharp partner!"

• • •

For Nita, fund-raising evolved into a program that required the stamina of a trained athlete, the skills of a personal shopper, and the tact of a counselor. By eleven P.M. Thursday evening, when she collapsed onto the sofa in the sitting room and kicked off her shoes to inspect the blisters she'd developed in the course of the hard day, she and Audrey McKinnon had toured the four skylit levels of the Eaton Center, progressed to the more rarefied environs of Creed's on Bloor Street, and recouped some strength over a luncheon of Camembert *beignets* with tomato sauce in Hazelton Lanes before tackling its popular boutiques offering everything from Hermès scarves to Davidoff cigars at over ten dollars apiece. Then they'd dined at Truffles, seen a French film, and spent an hour in a transplanted English pub on College and Yonge. At least during the film Nita had been able to sit down.

Matt's backpack and several maps lay strewn over one of the beds—not, she noted with a sigh, the one in the room containing her stacks of luggage—but she had no idea where he might be. He'd propped a note beside the phone on her night table: "If you have time, call Mrs. Lang (Mrs. Tech Corp., Room 706) and Mrs. Hughes (Noranda Development, Room 1141). Your fame spreads."

Evidently he'd reconciled himself to her help; although, as she crawled into bed, the victory rang a little hollow. At this rate, those romantic candlelit dinners she'd planned might all turn out to be hen parties.

On Friday Nita left Audrey a personally selected list of the best antique shops in town, arranged for Mrs. Tech Corp. to have her hair styled at one of the fashionably kinky hair salons on Markham Street, supervised the purchase of gifts for Mrs. Noranda Development's many grandchildren, and accompanied the now sleekly coiffed and radiant Mrs. Tech Corp. on a cultural tour that included stops at the art gallery and Grange, the Sigmund Samuel collection of Canadiana, and several footsore hours examining textiles and Oriental art at the ROM, known to the uninitiated as the Royal Ontario

Museum. Leaving her to wow Mr. Tech Corp. with her new image and hopefully to spend the kind of evening Nita once had in mind for herself and Matt, she joined Audrey for dinner in the courtyard café of the nearby Windsor Arms Hotel, then spent the evening amid the delights of Ontario Place with Mrs. Noranda Development, whose grandchildren had requested an in-depth description. The note she left Matt that night read: "Cocktails tomorrow at six. I have indigestion and fallen arches. I hope you've had success."

The next morning Mrs. Tech Corp. slept late, and Nita envied her. Between fighting the Saturday morning mob around the outdoor stalls at the Kensington Market so Audrey could fly back to Vancouver in her husband's private plane with multiple pounds of smelly cheeses acquired at bargain prices, lunching on dim sum at the Pink Pearl on the fringes of Chinatown, and ferrying Mrs. Noranda Development to Centre Island so that she could see the children's zoo, Nita managed to fill her day. None of the backers' wives showed any interest in the opening game of the baseball season. Only Matt might have understood how happily Nita would have traded all the city's greater glories for an afternoon watching the Toronto Blue Jays play.

When she returned to the suite at four-thirty, a faint fragrance of flowers filled the sitting room. The caterers had been busy laying the groundwork for the cocktail hour. Matt, as usual, was nowhere to be seen. She poured a luxurious amount of oil in her bath to eradicate the aromas of the children's zoo, and washed her hair to return the mop of curls created by a damp ferry ride to its normal satin luster. She was bending over the washbasin to brush her teeth, wearing only a sarong of terry toweling, with more of the same swathed around her head, when Matt steamed through the bathroom door.

"Sorry!"

"Ron't-mine-me," she said through a foam of toothpaste. "I-ronly-rork-rere."

He laughed. Grabbing a glass of water, she rinsed her mouth while staring at the vivid masculine features reflected in the mirror. His expression could mean only one of two things—terry cloth was the ultimate in seductive at-home wear, or Lamartine-Holiday Development was in terrific shape. Her spirits rose and she turned around. "Is all that glee because our paths haven't crossed for three days and you're so glad to see me?"

"Among other things."

Pulling her against him, he kissed her roundly on the mouth. Then he drew away slightly, changed his mind, pushed the door shut with one foot, and gathered her back for another prolonged kiss. The hope of candlelight dining was revived once more by the hunger with which his lips clung to hers, urging a response she gave without reserve. Linking her arms around his neck, she threaded her fingers through his shaggy black hair in caresses that echoed the tremors running from her head down to her bare toes. His impassioned embrace kneaded the knot of her sarong into a dangerous stage of disorder. Neither of them noticed until the clank and rattle of the caterer's carts in the next room announced the approach of six o'clock. When Matt lifted his head his eyes were slightly glazed and softened by the intensity of their contact. "Got to dress," he said, although his lips began to wander down her neck.

"Ex-models are very fast," she murmured, "at dressing."

His mouth reached her shoulder and for several minutes the thoroughness with which he explored its contours distracted them from anything but the keen sensation of flesh on flesh. "Got to dress," he repeated.

"Mmm." She stroked his hair without opening her eyes.

He nudged aside the already loosened towel with his lips, fanning his passage with breaths from deep inside his chest. Her breasts rose and fell in a jagged response. "Got to dress," he said, groaning.

"Or else undress."

"Wouldn't be in the family's interests."

She trembled slightly as his lips advanced. "I wouldn't let on. I'm here in a private capacity."

"People more or less expect their hosts to turn up at their own party," he said in a muffled voice. "Especially if they plan to offer them money."

"They're going to offer?"

"Mmm."

She gasped as his murmuring lips grazed her sensitized skin. "Then we ought to be thinking of our long-term goals."

"Nita . . ."

She moaned. "Got to get dressed."

"Later."

"Now . . ."

"Mmm."

"Instantly," she cried as his mouth opened on its goal. She caught his face between her hands, planted a kiss on his parted lips, grabbed her drooping towel, and fled to her room.

"I'll be signing papers worth thousands in a state of pain," he called after her.

"They can't stay forever!"

The party was marvelous. Nita floated through it in a glow as golden as her lamé gown, but the mood seemed general. Optimism filled the air. Good humor bubbled and burst into laughter on all sides. Although her attention was focused on Matt like a magnet pointing to true north, her guests found her concentration on him natural because tonight he was golden in their eyes as well. The confidence she'd helped create had taken hold. If anyone could stake out hidden reserves of ore less than five hundred miles from where they stood, no one doubted Matthew Lamartine was the man.

At seven forty-five Pez McKinnon drew Matt into one of the bedrooms. Bonhomie became business. When they returned, Matt's scowl looked positively ferocious beside the McKinnon smile. Nita's heart began to pound. Something had gone wrong.

Pez drained the last half-inch of whiskey from his glass and set it down with a rattle of ice cubes. "Drink up, Audrey. Time to get back into harness. Don't want the competition to steal a march on us."

"We're not flying back tonight!" she exclaimed.

"Can't start too soon. Had to squelch a couple of rumors on my way up here."

"Way off the mark, I hope?" said Mr. Tech Corp.

"Not far enough."

Mr. Noranda Development frowned at Matt. "Expect there'll be some snooping around, then."

"Pez thinks we'll be safe if I'm the first off the mark," Matt said grimly.

"Going to drop him off so he can pack up," Pez said. "He travels light enough so I won't have to choose between taking him or the wife.' The gold-capped McKinnon molars glinted as he laughed. "If we let him stay, I'm not sure he'd get to work at all!"

Nita froze. "You're flying to Houghton tonight?" she asked Matt.

"I've four months' worth of supplies to organize, Nita. And the forty-five percent comes with its own strings attached."

"But we—"

Pez McKinnon's massive hand held her back. "No use arguing. Equipping a Canadian trip from the States is a lot of damn foolishness and red tape. Bound to slow things down. You folks in Chicago might be in this thing for the hell of it, but mining's our business. Matt knows that. We made only one condition. Our man doesn't come in second at the claims office."

"Of course." She managed a smile. "I understand."

"That's the spirit. You get him to take you out in the bush sometime. After we file," he added with another roar of laughter, clapping Matt on the shoulder. "See you in the lobby in forty-five minutes, boy. I've got Audrey trained, so don't you hold me up."

His wife took the assignment of packing up the booty from three days' hard shopping on a moment's notice in her stride. "Mining men live like sailors, dearie," she said as she pecked Nita's cheek. "But you get used to it. And all the coming and going keeps the pep in a relationship, if you know what I mean."

Shock kept Nita's smile intact during the thanks and farewells, but when she closed the door and turned to Matt, she couldn't hide the disappointment in her voice. "This mine is ruining my life, you know that?"

"Nita, I have no choice."

"Why couldn't you refuse to go until tomorrow?"

"I did! But you saw how Pez reacted just now. The more I objected, the more determined he was to fly me out tonight. As you might have noticed, money gets the last word."

"Damn that Russell!" she exclaimed. "What can you do in Houghton? You won't get hold of him before tomorrow. He's probably in the Bahamas!"

Matt grinned faintly. "Somehow I bet he'll rise to this challenge."

"But flying a private plane at night is suicidal! What are they trying to do? Eliminate you and go out themselves?"

"Pez has had his license since he was twenty-one."

"You have all the answers, don't you?" She hugged herself against a chilling tide of frustration and balked hopes. "Sometimes I wonder whose side you're on."

In two strides he was beside her, roughly pinioning her arms. "Dammit, Nita! Only an ultimatum could make me leave. You know that. I'm hamstrung every way. I have to go."

"I ordered champagne for us."

"When I get back we'll have it by the bathtubful."

"Actually indulge in little decadent privacy?"

"How about a lot?"

Slipping her arms around his waist, she pressed her face into the lapel of his jacket. His body softened in welcome as he gathered her close. "Sounds fantastic," she murmured, "but I have a better idea."

"Pez is right, Nita. If I stayed tonight, I'd never leave."

"But I could go."

He pulled back, puzzled. "What do you mean?"

"Go with you next week."

For a moment, in the unguarded depths of his brown eyes, she caught the flicker of a vision like her own: four months in which to learn all that time could teach them about loving each other. "Nita . . ." He stopped himself with an effort. "No, the idea's crazy."

"Why?"

"I'll be going miles into the bush."

"Think of the time we'd have together."

"This isn't a pleasure trip."

"Nobody can work twenty-four hours a day."

"I couldn't ask you to rough it in the wilderness for months." He swallowed. "No matter how much I wanted you along."

"I'm volunteering."

"It's impossible," he said hurriedly. "You know nothing about prospecting, nothing about camping. I'll be packing in every item I use, walking more miles in a day than you walk in two weeks— "

"Fine! Good exercise. Fresh air." She grinned. "Choice company."

"Maybe if the life weren't so hard . . ."

"I can handle it. You might not have been around enough lately to notice, but I'm in terrific shape."

He groaned. "I've noticed."

"And the gym in my apartment isn't for decoration." She flexed her biceps. "Look at that."

"Could you carry sixty pounds all day?"

Although she had no clear idea of poundage, she didn't hesitate. "Yes."

"Walk thirty miles?"

"Why not?"

"And be fit for anything afterward?"

"What did you have in mind?" she purred.

"I'm serious, Nita. You'd have to run the crusher, clean fish, pitch a tent— "

"Under the stars."

The dark eyes wavered for an instant. "Look, you heard what Pez said. I can't afford to let anything— anyone—slow me down."

"He was joking."

"Pez has one thing in common with your family. He doesn't joke about money. Seeing us together was enough to tip him off about how much work I'd do with you around."

"Be fair, Matt. I haven't been in your way this weekend. How many times do I have to prove myself? We're partners, remember? If Aunt Addy heard you objecting like this, she'd think you had something to hide."

"Nita, for Lord's sake!"

"Then prove you're not planning something underhanded. Take me along."

"Is this blackmail?"

"No," she said sweetly. "It's another ultimatum."

"Now wait a minute." Holding her at arm's length, he studied her face. "Let's get this completely straight. You can't change your mind once our plane drops us off."

"I wouldn't want to."

"Don't expect to be pampered."

She smiled at him. "I'll clean half the fish."

"Would you really come?"

"Yes."

"Sure?"

"Ask me."

For an instant he hesitated, his jaw clenched with the effort of balancing between denial and desire. But molten points of light flared in his eyes, and when he drew her into his arms a husky softness in his voice promised a search for greater wealth than gold. "I am asking you," he said.

Six

Nita pinned the phone receiver against her ear with her shoulder in order to dig more quarters out of her purse. At the other end of the line Libby's sleepy voice sounded farther away than New York. "Nita? What's wrong? It's only six-thirty."

"No use expecting pity from me. It's four-thirty here, I've been up half the night, the temperature is thirty-five degrees on June first, and although my behavior seems uncivilized, I waited as long as I could. I really did."

"Where's here? The Antarctic?"

"Thunder Bay."

"Should that mean something?"

"Maybe not to a native New Yorker. It's where Air Canada, Nord Air, and Bearskin Air Lines intersect." The shelf of the phone booth dug into the small of Nita's back as she rotated to survey her surroundings with distaste: three desks and a baggage rack were the small room's only furnishings, and two stolid Ojibwa Indians the only other customers. "I'm standing in what they claim is an airport."

"Dare I ask why?"

"As soon as Matt gets here, we're going after the gold."

"You're kidding!"

"Romantic, huh?"

"Just the two of you?"

Nita's mouth spread into a smile. "Mmm."

"That part sounds romantic," Libby said cautiously,

"but I thought prospecting meant roughing it. Somehow I can't picture you traveling without a stream of porters and reservations at the local Hilton."

Through the windows of the low building Nita could see that the early morning light had brightened enough to reveal encircling pine trees, the small plane that had brought her from Chicago, a rickety flight of metal stairs still pulled up to its side, and the ground crew piling the last of her suitcases onto a towering stack.

"I cut back to the bare essentials," she said. "Matt doesn't want me to slow him down."

"Sounds more like a heist than a search."

"Not a heist, a coup. Let me tell you, this trip is so secret it could have been planned by the CIA. All I know is that from here Bearskin Air drops us off near some lake and we trek in, probably brushing over our tracks, crossing rivers to throw off the dogs, and all that stuff. The backers are afraid someone might beat us to the claim."

"You mean you're going to camp? In the bush?"

"For about four months," Nita said with a sigh.

"You must be crazy!"

"Matt's prospecting all summer. What else could I do?"

"I suppose you rejected the obvious solution of waiting for him to come back?"

"For sixteen weeks?"

"I know the feeling." Libby's smile carried into her voice. "He must be crazy about you too. You're the last person a *sane* man would take with him into the wilderness."

"I think I resent that."

"I don't doubt he craves your company, but has he ever seen the way you travel? The number of *romances* you'd need for four months would weigh a hundred pounds."

"All I packed," Nita said virtuously, "were a couple of books on prospecting and Euell Gibbons on wild foods."

"If Gibbons had written a book on cosmetic plants, you could lighten up by another twenty or thirty pounds."

"Oh, come on. I'm only taking a blow dryer, some creams, a little lip gloss, one or two—"

Libby began to laugh.

"And I'm not paying to listen to you chuckle in that ghoulish fashion. I simply wanted to tell you to write me in care of Russell, because he's arranging the supply drops."

"Your brother Russell? I hate to say it, friend, but this trip sounds doomed."

Overhead, the drone of an approaching plane grew louder as it circled the building. The Indians moved over to the window. Nita's pulse began to thump. "Look, Matt's plane is landing. I have to run. Wish me luck!"

"I wish you more than that. If you survive, send us a prospectus so we can invest in the mine. And an invitation to the wedding!"

"Survive? I plan to flourish!"

Without pausing to put on her jacket after she hung up the phone, Nita ran toward the light plane taxiing to a stop. As she waited impatiently for Matt to appear, her breath formed white clouds in the air, but the cold and early hour was forgotten when his lean body appeared in the doorway. He jumped lightly to the ground and swept her shivering frame into a one-armed hug.

"Made the first lap okay?" he asked.

"I probably forgot my toothbrush."

He laughed. "If Russell sent the supplies I ordered, we'll get along."

"You'll shave me a nifty replacement out of twigs, right?"

"Basic Woodcraft B."

"Sounds like you're in your element."

"Nearly. But your teeth are chattering."

She shook her head. His partner had to be tough, not fragile. He'd made that clear. Although she hadn't bargained for freezing temperatures, she wasn't about to complain. "Must be the effect you have on me."

"Then you'd better come in here where it's warm."

As he held open his jacket, a promise of their first night together crept into the husky timbre of his voice, and in spite of her resolve to be strong, his protective gesture beckoned with irresistible appeal. No need to *exaggerate* her independence. Slipping her arm around his waist, she snuggled against the warmth of his body and matched her stride to his.

From the hangar end of the building a plane rolled down the tarmac toward them. It was smaller than the one in which Matt had arrived, and made Nita's Air Canada from Chicago look like a 747. Even painting a name as long as Bearskin Air Lines on its sides must have presented a challenge. When it stopped beside Nita's mound of luggage, it looked smaller still.

"That must be ours," Matt said.

"Do we do the next lap wind surfing?"

"Lighter is cheaper."

"Not," she said with heavy sarcasm, "if we have to take one each."

The pilot lifted the bubble dome over his craft's snout, clambered out across one wing, and headed for the building. "You the folks going to the lodge?" he asked. "Be about twenty minutes."

His reference to a lodge came as a cheerful surprise to Nita. Any romance reader knew wilderness lodges meant roaring fires, brandy snifters, fur rugs, and uncontrollable passions. That was worth riding in what looked like a balsa-wood model to reach.

"We'd better load up," Matt said. "Where's your stuff? Inside?"

"No. That's it. Beside the plane."

He frowned. "For Pete's sake, what did Russell do, pack everything as though he were shipping Chinese antiques?"

"The two cartons are what he sent. The rest is mine."

"Eight square feet?"

Feeling him stiffen, she eased out of his warm jacket and swallowed hard. "I cut down as much as I could."

"Nita, we're *backpacking*."

"I know, but—"

"You planned to harness a couple of moose to pull a wagon?"

"Surely we can find some people—"

"That's a great idea," he said grimly. "Hire *bearers!*

And on the way back they can clear a trail for the competition!" He ran one hand through his hair before his exasperation subsided enough for him to give her a crooked grin. "Sorry. I shouldn't blame you. I knew you couldn't possibly visualize what you were getting into, but I wanted you with me too much to admit you couldn't handle a trip like this. Agreeing to bring you along was pure wish fulfillment."

"I'll repack," she said hastily. "Give me ten minutes."

"Can't risk it."

"Five minutes. Would you have told the Wright brothers to give up flying because their first design crashed?"

"Your luggage isn't the problem. It simply proves what I should have faced from the beginning."

"What?"

He put his arms around her as though her stretch jeans and flannel shirt hid a core of glass. "Nita, living in the woods is a dangerous business if you don't know what you're doing. It was crazy to imagine you could pick up the skills you need by some kind of osmosis just so I could justify taking you along. You're too precious to me to put in jeopardy because I can't face being apart."

"You mean you're backing out?"

"I'm *not* backing out." Frowning, he released her. "I'm responsible for you. Can't you see that?"

"You'll be gone for months!"

"Dammit, don't argue! Do you think I want to leave you?"

"I can take care of myself."

"Sure you can—at a cocktail party or in a board room. Face facts, Nita. You can't outtalk a bear or make a deal with a rutting moose. Comfort and safety aren't for sale where we're going; experience is all that counts. Anything could happen to you on a trip like this."

Dangerous animals didn't figure into the encounters that flashed through her mind—except for the fur rug on which she and Matt were lying. But he was right about one thing. Nothing would happen if she let him leave her behind.

"I trust you enough to go," she pleaded. "Why can't you trust me back?"

"Nita . . ."

"I'm a quick learner."

He groaned. "Stop looking at me like that."

"I'm also motivated."

"You've never faced being on your own in the wild."

"I wouldn't be alone. I'd be with you."

His hand clenched around the strap of his pack. "Look, it's for your sake I'm fighting you on this. Do you have any idea how much I counted on our time together?"

"So did I."

"You'll be miserable."

"Only if you leave without me."

"After we land you'll wish I'd talked some sense into you."

"Not tonight," she said softly.

Their eyes held for a long moment before he shook his head, a dazed expression on his face. "So it's up to me to make your suffering worthwhile?"

"Not all alone." She smiled. "Fifty-fifty was the deal we made."

He let out his breath with a strangled laugh. "Okay. It's hopeless for me to try to fight you. Those moose will have to fend for themselves. Why is it," he added, sweeping her into a bone-crunching hug that circled her high into the air, "every time I let you beat up my better judgment I suddenly feel terrific?"

"Must be significant."

He kissed the tip of her nose before he let her feet touch the ground again. "Cut down your stuff. I'll check about shipping back the rest."

"You got it, partner!"

She started hauling bags from the stack. Going along meant going without, but how did one revise an entire philosophy of dress in less than ten minutes? Did he really expect her to wear one pair of jeans and the red-and-blue plaid shirt on her back for four straight months? Her fingers worked as fast as her mind, and the phrase "bare essentials" took on vivid new meaning. Luxury might be out, but silk T-shirts folded up small and unfolded sexy. Hiking boots and some mole-skin foot plasters would underpin a smile after thirty miles of walking. The hair dryer was an early discard. The nail polish remover stayed.

When Matt returned with her jacket wadded under his arm and business in his eye, she sat back on her haunches and pointed to her compact result with pride. "I guess the plane ought to be able to take off now," she said.

As he ripped into Russell's cartons with an efficiency that made her eyes widen, his smile rewarded her. "See if you can fit it all in here," he said, tossing her a pack so elaborated with double-zippered compartments, web-bing loops, and padded straps it suggested moon walks rather than the lodge life she imagined. "I'll show you how to load up properly before we start walking."

Out of the corner of her eye she watched him trans-fer the contents of his light pack to a larger twin of the one he'd given her. With the finesse of a champion grocery bagger, he added a bewildering array of uten-sils, pocket binoculars, flashlights, foodstuffs, and safety equipment. Unlike her own misshapen effort, when he finished his pack looked smooth and tight.

From the last carton he extracted several pristine, blue-bagged rolls. "Strap your sleeping bag and foam pad to the bottom." He demonstrated by fastening some worn cylinders onto his own pack.

"What are those? Spares?"

"The top one's our tent."

Her idyllic image of their accommodations dwindled perceptibly. Tents were not lodges. Not by a long shot. But she accepted her blue rolls without a murmur. In romances, sleeping bags existed to be shared.

The pilot emerged from the office, followed by the two Indians who climbed into the cabin of the plane with the aplomb of frequent flyers. "If you're all set," the pilot yelled to Matt and Nita, "climb aboard."

The plane took off with a shuddering effort that tight-ened Nita's damp hands into fists. Straining along with its engines, she regretted the jars of face cream she'd stuffed into her pack at the last minute and felt a rush of gratitude toward the Indians for carrying no luggage at all. Whether their plane would clear the tops of the pines remained in doubt until the final seconds of takeoff. Even if her heart hadn't been in her mouth, conversation was impossible over the noise. No hostess to pass out gum either. Or a calming drink.

Below, on her right, the tongues of land sheltering Thunder Bay drifted out of view and the icy water of Lake Superior stretched away to the horizon. After what seemed like hours of bumping through air no gentler than a road full of potholes, Matt yelled from across the aisle, "Trans-Canada Highway coming up on the left."

"Will the plane tip over if I take a look?"

He grinned and held out his hand. As the margin of the lake passed beneath them, the expanse of blue turned into endless stretches of knobby, dark-green forest, broken occasonally by a system of streams and lakes that glinted like flares as they caught the early sunlight. A dull sliver of highway threaded its lonely path along the shoreline of the lake.

"Gorgeous country, isn't it?" Matt shouted.

She managed a smile. "Not one backyard swimming pool in the whole place."

Their descent was no less terrifying than the takeoff, and the spot where they landed made Thunder Bay airport seem as posh as O'Hare. A patch of grass, a shed, and a single electric pole made her respect the pilot's skill in finding their destination at all.

The two Ojibwa said something incomprehensible to Matt and received a laconic reply. Then they got out and vanished between the trees. After dumping both packs on the ground, the pilot clambered back over the wing into his seat and lifted his hand to pull down the bubble cover. "Have a good one!" he called. "Hear the fish are biting over on the Pukaskwa."

"Swell," Matt yelled back.

The plane grew smaller in the distance and finally disappeared altogether. Although Matt fastened his dark gaze on Nita's face, watching for her response with an intensity she sensed like a physical touch, a sense of isolation engulfed her. Instinctively she moved closer to him.

He put his arm around her. "Are you okay?"

"Me?" She smiled thinly. "Great."

But even the knowledge that they were alone at last—and gifted with a wealth of time they'd never shared before—didn't ease her feeling of dislocation. Thick forest enclosed them on all sides—vast, dappled only by pale slivers of light, and as still as though devoid of life. The two Indians might have been figments of her imagination.

"You'll grow to love the quiet," he said.

"Yes?" She wasn't so sure. Clearing her throat, she gestured toward the spot where she had seen the Indians last. "Do they live around here?"

"There's a provincial reserve about seven miles away."

"Practically neighbors."

He laughed. "Not exactly, but near enough so some of the tribe work as guides at the sporting lodge where we're supposedly staying."

The byplay about lodges and fish fell into place. He'd been covering their trail. "You should have told me to look like an angler."

"So you could wear color-coordinated waders?"

"Are you making fun of the way I'm dressed?"

"Nope." He grinned. "The fit is a treat."

"Wait until you see my après tent-pitching wear. Under the new regime it's what you might describe as skintight."

"I knew making you lighten your pack was a smart idea."

"And I thought you were worried about my stamina!"

He glanced up at the sky as though some kind of information were written in its azure emptiness, and a frown replaced his smile. He bent to heave his pack into place on his shoulders. "I am. Think you can walk twenty miles before noon?"

"Are you kidding?"

"No."

"I didn't mean I couldn't," she corrected herself hastily.

"What's a measly twenty miles to a stouthearted woman?"

They seemed closer to forty before the morning was over. Hindered by the bulk of her pack as much as by its weight, she crashed through the underbrush behind Matt like an elephant trailing an antelope. How he figured out where they were headed was a complete mystery to her. There was no path, every tree looked exactly like the others, yet he forged ahead as though they were following markers through a state park. If she hadn't been concentrating so hard on saving some strength for later, she would have been even more impressed.

When they finally stopped beside a lake longer and narrower than those they had passed, she collapsed on the ground without looking around or even unbuckling her load. "Did we make it?" she asked, gasping.

"Almost. We'll still reach the base camp by late afternoon."

"You mean this isn't *it?*"

"Lunch break."

Only the prospect of convivial relaxation had kept her going for the last few miles, but she controlled her disappointment the best she could, settling for beef broth from his thermos, cheese on whole wheat, and the pleasure of leaning back against his chest while she ate. He peeled a couple of oranges and fed her sections for quick energy. She accepted them with closed eyes, melting deeper into the cradle of his arms. Half-dozing to the steady drumming of his heart beneath her ear, she returned to consciousness with the pressure of his mouth on hers.

"Is this on our schedule?" she asked contentedly.

"No, but I couldn't resist."

"Ten more minutes?"

"Pushing too hard might be counterproductive."

She smiled back at him and put her arms around his neck. "You're the boss."

By the time their positions evolved enough for Matt's weight to begin pressing a gnarled root and several small rocks into her back, she'd decided kissing was her tonic of choice for fatigue. Orange sections didn't even come close. But when she lifted slightly and blinked into the sun, its new angle was apparent even to her amateur eyes.

"Matt?"

"Uncomfortable? I'll get out one of the pads."

"I think the ten minutes might be over."

He glanced at the sky. Brushing a tousled strand of hair back from her face, he said huskily, "We could camp here."

"We'd lose a day."

"Yup."

She swallowed. "I . . . promised I wouldn't hold you back. What if somebody's on our trail?"

"It's a risk."

The shadow that crossed his face decided her. No regrets. That's what they'd promised each other from the beginning. She didn't want anything to go wrong now. "Is it much farther?"

"Fifteen miles."

"Fifteen?" Dismay crept into her voice.

"Up to it?"

"You can kiss me if I start to flag."

"We'd land in the lake." He gave her a wry look. "The last lap's by canoe."

"Great." With a determined smile, she struggled to a sitting position and surveyed the canoeless shore. "Does it rise up out of the water like King Arthur's sword, or simply sail across under its own power like Lohengrin's swan boat?"

"It's back in the brush. Friends of mine paddled it over. They store my heavy equipment during the winter."

She stared at him, too surprised to move. "You have friends here?"

"Some."

"Indians? Like those two on the plane? You really understood what they said?"

"I speak some Ojibwa."

"I hope that's not one of the necessary survival tools."

"For them maybe," he said quietly. "Not for you."

"Will I meet them? I mean later?"

"Maybe. Look, Nita—"

The urgency with which he caught her arm took her by surprise. "What's wrong?"

"Tell me you're not sorry you came."

"I'm not." She hesitated. "Are you?"

"How could I be?"

"For a minute, I wondered. You looked so strange."

"Sometimes I'm scared to death I'll lose you." His grasp slid down to her hand and tightened on it. "Come on. We'd better get moving. If we're going to fall into the lake I'd rather do it in daylight."

She smiled, but the moment stayed with her, nagging like an unsolved puzzle while they loaded their packs into the canoe, along with army shovels, picks, drills, sample bags, hatchets, and axes, which had been neatly stowed beside it. She tried to push her uneasiness aside. So what if he trusted some Indians with the destination he'd refused to share with her? It was logical to make Indian friends in Indian country. To him hesitating about letting her meet them probably seemed logical too. Only a mind like Aunt Addy's would find the fact suspicious.

Matt showed her how to paddle. The principle of using her body weight rather than her arm muscles seemed simple, but his demonstration, which involved folding his arms around her while his bronzed hands guided hers and their bodies moved together, was so agreeable she indulged in a certain denseness about catching onto it. In practice, however, the liquid ease of his movement was impossible to match on her own. Her jerky strokes splashed water all over them, caused the canoe to bob disconcertingly, and sent them on a ragged course. Did the fifteen miles he'd mentioned include zigzagging all over the lake? she wondered.

"Easy, there," he said. "Let me do the work."

"I'm going to do my share," she muttered, putting so much force into her jab-and-plunge technique she spun them off into a fresh circle.

"Steering isn't your job," he said dryly. "Listen for my stroke. Canoeing is part rhythm, part telepathy."

Like several other two-person activities she could mention. Well, if sexy canoeing was what he wanted, she'd show him some virtuoso work. Taking a deep breath, she rested her paddle lightly across the bow, every sense alert to him. Without looking back, she knew he rested too.

Listening so intently, she became aware of her surroundings for the first time. All around them, pines and firs marched down to the curving borders of the lake, blackening the golden-brown water with their shadows. Here and there birches clustered in a clearing where their white trunks caught the sun. The deep, isolating stillness that had oppressed her when they first arrived dissolved into a thousand subtle signals: water licking the sides of the canoe, the hum of a dragonfly, the sigh and rustle of the wind.

"Pretty here, isn't it?" she said with sudden pleasure.

"You'll like the campsite. I use it every year."

He lifted his paddle and the boat shot forward as the blade cut through the water. It broke the surface with a gentle slurp at the end of the stroke and cast a trail of droplets as he swung it around to cut again. For a few moments she let the rhythm seep into her, then took up her own paddle and matched her movements to his. Their path straightened like magic. Suddenly they were gliding.

"Hey! Look, Ma, I'm canoeing!"

He laughed. "Now all you have to do is keep it up for another fourteen and seven-eighths miles."

She did, but by the time he directed the canoe toward a point beyond the mouth of a small river, where the pines thinned and a margin of marshy grasses gave way to solid, open land, her arms were as tired as her legs. If she hadn't been in good shape before she started, she wouldn't have had enough energy left to groan.

"Have to hustle," Matt said. "We're losing the light. Let me show you around first. The river's for drinking and washing."

In spite of her aching thighs and calves she knelt to

dip her fingers in the water. It was cold enough to induce heart failure on contact with seldom-exposed skin.

"Last year," he continued, "I built a weir farther up. When you're out this long you have to eat off the land as much as you can. If my trap weathered the winter, we'll have fish for dinner tonight."

Striding across the rocks with surefooted grace, he was almost out of sight before she could scramble to her feet and follow. By the time she leaped, hopped, and splashed her way upstream to the weir, he had moved a log into place at the opening of the V-shaped barrier and trimmed a few light poles to lay beneath it. "After they jump clear of the log," he explained, "the fish simply flop around on these dry poles."

"Until you come by to pick them up?" Since the whole process had taken him no longer than it would have taken her to bait a hook, she felt justified in gaping. "You weren't kidding about wilderness survival tactics, were you?"

"Pole fishing is for vacationers."

"Chicago people?"

"Yup." He grinned at her. The light was fading quickly now, and she limped after him as he headed into the woods. "Commode's in that direction. Just pick a friendly bush. There's a little poison ivy, though. Better take a flashlight at night."

She groaned inwardly. Trying to fix some landmark for the inevitable return visit, she crashed into him when he suddenly stopped on the edge of the clearing with one arm outstretched to bar her way. "What's the matter?" she gasped.

"Look."

"At what?"

"There's a nest."

Peering upward into the gathering gloom, she muttered, "I don't see anything."

"No, over there. In the grasses," he whispered, taking her hand. "Giant Canadas sometimes build on old muskrat houses. If we're careful, we can go closer. The female usually leaves her eggs for a few minutes about this time of day."

On top of the abandoned muskrat mound five spheres gleamed in a down-lined ring of twigs and sticks. Matt's gesture and pressure on her hand drew her attention to a pair of large gray birds with white cheeks and necks like black swans gliding through the water toward the nest.

Matt seemed so struck by their arrival, she waited first on one foot, then the other for the naturalist's thrill to wear off. They were enormous birds all right, but at this rate her legs might not hold up until she could lie down. A full half-minute passed before she said, "I hate to tell you your business, but it's getting dark. Don't we have more important things to do?"

At the sound of her voice, the male reared in alarm. Even to an inexpert eye, his wingspan passed six feet. The thing was colossal and the husky endearment with which he had greeted his returning mate turned into loud honks of aggression.

Matt's hand checked her instinctive retreat. "He'll get used to us. Giant Canadas are pretty easygoing with humans."

"Why don't we give him time to adjust in private?"

"I thought you were a romantic."

"What's so romantic about an attack bird in a swamp?"

He smiled. "Those are *geese*."

"Geese?" Her eyes widened in comprehension. "You mean, the ones that mate for life?"

"And they chose our spot."

Their eyes met and his hand tightened on hers. The light wavered between rose and lavender, the moment when harsh edges fade into softness, a few stars begin to glow in the pale sky, and the air grows sweeter and seems to sing. Her shoes were gradually filling with water, but what did it matter?

"If you're planning to kiss me," she murmured, "could we move to dry land?"

Matt glanced at the horizon. Evidently this time the

invisible message in the sky read curfew. "I am. But first we'd better get you fed and dry."

He had the tent set up and his gear stowed inside before she figured out how to unstrap her sleeping bag. But when he brought back the fish, cleaned them, built a fire, spitted them on thin sticks to broil, and she was still struggling to free it from its blue sack, his looks grew too pointed to ignore.

"Can't seem to undo this sack," she said.

"Bring it over nearer the light. I'll do it. It's perfectly simple. . . ." He tugged at the cords, then frowned and tugged harder. Finally, he eased his pocketknife out of his jeans. Ten minutes later blue vinyl remains of the demolished sleeping bag surrounded them. "If this is a typical sample of the supplies your brother sent, we're in big trouble."

"What went wrong?"

"He squeezed seam sealant into all the channels."

"Don't worry. Russell's selective. He wouldn't sabotage any crucial equipment."

"You think your sleeping bag's not crucial?"

She shook her head, smiling. "Those geese only built one nest."

Seven

Although exhaustion already weighted Nita's eyelids, sitting in the darkness after supper, watching the dying fire with a mug of hot tea warming her hands, and familiar folk songs blending Matt's voice with hers, she wouldn't have changed places with another person in the world. As he leaned forward to stir the ashes a burst of flame highlighted the carved planes of Matt's face, the supple strength of fingers clasped around his cup, the triangle of moles on his jaw. Gathering cold at her back and the pull of his presence drew her closer, but she couldn't risk resting her head on his shoulder. Sleep wasn't the reward she'd waited so long to win.

"Bet you've forgotten this one," he said. His mellow voice picked up the lilting rhythm of a sixties song about forsaking city life.

" 'And I'm gon-na be a coun-try girl a-gain,' " she finished with him. "Buffy Sainte-Marie! The first time I heard her sing I wanted to get myself one of those Indian mouth-bows and take to the woods."

"This is your chance."

"Four whole months." She sighed with contentment. "Who taught you so much about living in the wild?"

"My mother."

"Your *mother*?" Surprise fluttered her eyes wide. "How did she know?"

He poured the dregs from his cup on the fire before he answered, and when he turned to her again the shadow in his eyes penetrated her weariness. Had he

ever mentioned his past without that look of strain?
She sat up straight.

"How *did* she, Matt?"

"She . . . taught at a reservation school. My brother
and I lived with her there."

"In the place you described? The one in Canada?"

"Yes."

"You never told me you lived with Indians."

He avoided her eyes. "Do you mind?"

"It would have helped me understand why you grew
up feeling like such an outsider."

"Would it?" His voice had a bitter edge. "I suppose I
could risk telling you the whole story now that you're
stuck in the wilderness. It's too late to change your
mind if you don't like what you hear."

She laid her hand on his arm. "The only thing I don't
like is your feeling that you can't be open with me.
That day in my apartment you called trust basic."

"I remember."

"You were right, you know."

"In theory."

"Matt, when are you going to stop thinking of me as
a plastic princess who's only interested in corporate
bloodlines? I'm a woman. I don't want you to be anyone but the man sitting beside me." She glanced at the
black unknown that began just beyond the embers of
the fire and shifted closer to him with a little smile and
a shiver. "I sure wouldn't want to be out here tonight
with somebody who grew up in Chicago."

"Nita, I can't joke about this."

"I know. But whatever happened back then doesn't
have to be the barrier you've created in your mind,
either. Maybe there's a reason why it's so hard for you to
talk about it, and I'll wait until you're ready, but you
could trust me. You *could*."

"I don't want to burden you with my problems."

"It hurts more to be shut out."

"I've never felt closer to anyone. You have to believe
that." Covering the hand resting on his arm with his
own, he drew in a deep breath before he turned to her.

"But I can't expect you to handle revelations on top of the day I've put you through."

"I'm getting my second wind."

He smiled faintly. "Let's not waste it talking."

Inside the sleeping bag Nita listened to the foreign noises of the night. Her resting place felt solid and unyielding beneath her, but neither strangeness nor discomfort was keeping her eyes wide open in the dark. No danger of falling asleep now. Matt's footsteps moved softly as he put the campsite in order, and every moment brought him closer to her.

He opened the tent flap at last. "You're not afraid?"

She shook her head, her mouth suddenly too dry for speech. He seemed to fill the tent with an energy that quickened every nerve of her body.

"Warm enough?" he asked.

"Mmm."

"Those geese have an easy time. All they do is find a nesting site."

"Nothing to it," she managed to croak. "No dishes to wash."

"They even mate in the water."

In stunned silence she evaluated the implications of this new bit of wilderness lore. Would he expect her to risk hypothermia for the sake of a romantic comparison? When she mated for life she had in mind more than one unforgettable night.

"It's a bit cold to try without feathers," he added.

"Whew," she gasped. "That's a relief!"

He laughed softly. The zipper slid down the side of their sleeping bag with a motion she sensed like a lick of fire. "Do I get any room?"

She shifted instantly. The movement triggered a sudden spasm in the weary muscle of her right calf. "Damn!" she cried, fumbling inside her cocoon to reach the pain.

"What's the matter?"

"My leg's cramped," she said through gritted teeth.

"Don't worry. It'll be gone in a minute. I won't turn fragile on you."

"Let me see."

He unzipped the bag completely, then straightened out her leg and began to knead the contracted muscle. As it relaxed, his strokes grew longer, extending to her instep and rising in lingering caresses to the tender spot behind her knee.

"Any better?"

"Yes, but don't stop."

"Would a massage make you fall asleep on me?"

"Are you kidding?"

"Then turn over," he said. "I don't want you laid up."

She didn't point out the illogic of linking a cramp in her leg to the rest of her body. In romances, back massages were usually described in steamy detail as a preliminary step to lovemaking. Until now she'd taken the accuracy of these reports on faith: the accelerated breathing, the erotic effect of the right pair of hands moving across the right parts of a person's body, desire rising steadily to unendurable heights. Matt certainly had the hero's touch. With a sigh of yearning—rising, but still blissfully endurable —she ignored the fact that long johns were never the heroine's costume on such occasions and abandoned herself to his ministrations.

"There's nothing to you," he said.

"Are you disappointed?" she asked anxiously. "Models are always scrawny."

"You're as delicate as a bird."

"Just keep thinking goose."

Tracing her contours more and more slowly, his hands roamed toward the hollow in the small of her back where her long john top and bottom overlapped. For a few moments his fingers outlined the join. Then they slid inside to caress her skin.

"That feels even better," she said.

"I thought it might."

The throaty purr in his voice made her swallow hard. "Let me get this out of your way."

With a model's expert motion she hitched out of her

top. Taking it from her, he tossed it aside, then gently turned her until she lay on her back. He continued to follow the fine-boned edge of her rib cage in complete silence for so long, her heartbeats seemed to shake her entire body. She took a deep breath. "Models are also sort of—of flat-chested. I guess that's not a figure problem for birds."

"You're beautiful," he said softly, cupping his hand lightly over her breast and circling its curves with his thumb. Her desire surged perceptibly upward, now both sweet and urgent. She caught the hand teasing her skin and slipped her other arm around his neck to draw his lips to hers.

"Matt . . ."

"I've wanted you so long."

Their mouths brushed, then opened on all the tender softness of a shared response whose power swelled and grew. With dizzying joy their kisses celebrated the double gifts of time and liberty. As her hands fretted at the clothing hiding his back and chest, he arched over her, flung aside his shirt, and returned to her mouth. When his naked flesh sank down against hers, his muffled groan drew her echo after it.

The sleek expanse of his back lay beneath her fingers, moving subtly as he let his torso graze over her tingling curves. Between caresses he freed their limbs of clothing, then intertwined them until nakedness itself became too slight a contact to satisfy their need. Shifting over her, he buried both hands in her hair, raining kisses on her closed lids and parted lips.

"I love you," he said in a voice that shook with intensity.

"Can you feel my heart beating?"

"I can't tell yours from mine."

She clasped him with a fierce exultation, shuddering as the bond that joined them pulsed through every vein and fiber. Endearments tumbled from their mouths between kisses, and when pleasure crested beyond speech, she, too—in the fullness of belonging to him—no longer knew his body from her own.

Her last drop of energy spent, she lay in the circle of his arm, drowsily caressing the smooth expanse of his chest as she listened to his heartbeat gradually slowing beneath her ear. "What do they do afterward?" she asked.

"Who?"

"The geese."

"Stretch their necks and rotate in the water until they're breast to breast."

"Ah."

His arm tightened around her. "Then the male lifts his wings and gives her an amorous version of his greeting cry."

"Afterplay." She raised her lips for another kiss. "How romantic."

"Then they throw water on their backs and swim ashore to preen."

"Pleased with themselves," she murmured.

"Mmm."

"I know the feeling."

"We could run through the whole routine sometime."

"In August," she said, smiling, "when the water's warmer."

The days that followed sang by under an unbroken succession of sunny skies. Some rain must have fallen, of course, for a haze of tender foliage slowly enveloped the birches and pale wild flowers sprang up from the pine-needled forest floor. But Nita left their tent each morning certain of Matt's love—if not his thoughts— and determined to gild the daylight hours with happiness.

Although they tramped the rocky outcrops and ridges west and north of their campsite laden with picks, hammers, shovels, and diamond drilling equipment, her steps were light. Even the plodding labor of digging test trenches every fifty feet across the strike lines he had projected during the previous summer strengthened her hope that the barriers he felt between them were destined to disappear.

While he swung a sledgehammer to chisel bits of rock from the exposed trench walls, she held the moil for his blow. He crushed the fragments. She learned how to pan them. By rotating the shallow pan with a deft motion as she lifted it from the water, she tipped away soil and gravel to leave what prospectors called colors—flakes of gold coiling in the bottom of the pan like a shimmering minnow's tail.

"Pretty soon," Matt said one day, watching her tuck her lower lip between her teeth in concentration, "I'll be able to enter you in the international panning contest."

She poured the dry results of an earlier sample into a canvas bag for the assayers. "Who's the champ?"

"A seventy-five-year-old from Sacramento. In twenty minutes he panned twenty chips of gold the size of pinheads from a ton of rocks."

"I couldn't move a ton of rocks in twenty minutes."

"Keep practicing," he said, laughing as he hooked a strand of her blond hair behind her ear.

She grew blasé about finding nuggets the size of grains of wheat in the bottom of her pan. Everything that glittered wasn't minable. A lode's value depended on ease of extraction as well as the proportion of ore to other minerals. As they continued to search for the all-important spout—the point where nature thrusts her grand prize into the prospector's hands—they drilled sample cores to test the depth and direction of every vein. Whenever the cores came out of the drill pipe showing patches of brownish-yellow thickly twined in quartz, the metal gleamed less brightly than the smiles of triumph they shared.

The nest also delivered up its daily progress report. On June fourth, five newly hatched goslings peeked out of the down beneath their mother's ample breast. Within a week their tawny bodies straightened and their tiny chests seemed to puff with accomplishment. They began to feed immediately, and while Nita learned to pan gold, the goslings learned to strip seeds from the marsh plants with a twist of their stumpy beaks. In two weeks they'd grown into leggy, teenaged geese, and she was impatient to show off the mine's success.

"Shouldn't we send some of these samples to the assayers?" she asked Matt.

"I'll take them into town in a day or so."

"Without me?" she asked in surprise.

Checking section lines on his charts seemed to absorb Matt's entire attention. "Wouldn't you like a day off?"

"I'd rather meet your friends."

"I'll bring you a souvenir," he said, pushing aside his papers to reach for her hand. But his reluctance to take her along stayed in her mind long after the pair of butter-soft moccasins he brought back became her footgear of choice around the camp and the mouth-bow he made for her a feature of their music-making.

At the end of June, when the goslings began to sport delicate wing feathers and dark brows over their bright eyes, Matt's second trip produced a roll of birchbark, from which he taught her how to craft bark dishes to be burned instead of washed after a meal, as well as a bat, a ball, and a catcher's mitt. Nita's uneasiness grew despite her pleasure. What didn't he want her to see in town?

Now, she anxiously waited for his return from his third trip, as if his physical presence were her only assurance that she wasn't losing him to some hidden power she couldn't understand. She watched the geese paddle home toward their nest through the red-gold extravagance of July's long evening light. Patches darkened the fuzzy necks of the young birds in anticipation of their parents' sleek black throats. The hands on nature's clock were flying round.

"You've been gone the longest ten hours of my life," she cried when Matt's canoe slid into grasping range and she could reach out to touch him again.

He took her gently in his arms. "Pining for civilization?"

"Only when you're away."

"Sure?"

"Sure."

Her head was resting against his shoulder, but she lifted it now to take in the panorama of firs that pointed toward the sky like arrows held in an invisible flèche, the crystalline water lapping gently at their feet, and the fiery grandeur of the western sky. For all its loveliness, the forest remained a foreign element, seemingly empty, yet teeming, as she was beginning to learn, with unknown life.

"I wish," she said, "I didn't need your arms around me to feel I belong here at all."

"That's my fault."

"No. I want more than you're ready to give me."

"I love you. Don't ever doubt that."

"Even when you're not here?"

He put his fingers under her chin to lift her face for his kiss. "No matter where I am."

Before their lips parted, the evening mist had begun to rise around the margin of the water. They hurried to unload the canoe, and he handed her a parcel the size and weight of a collection of feather pillows. "I brought you a surprise," he said.

"Oh, Matt!" Dropping everything else, she tore open the brown paper wrapping. A mountain of white flecked with gray gleamed in the fading light. Mixed emotions forgotten in delight, she drew out a large blanket and buried her arms and face in the fur. "It feels like a piece of cloud!"

"It's an old Ojibwa craft. They weave strips of tanned rabbit skin to make it soft on both sides."

"We'll have to try it out."

He smiled at her. "Exactly what I had in mind."

But as she gathered up the drift of fur to carry it to their tent, her doubts returned. Either she never left his thoughts, no matter how much time he spent in town, or he'd replaced the chip on his shoulder with a terrific guilty conscience.

Two more weeks of hard work produced another batch of sample bags for the assayers and strengthened her resolve not to let Matt take them into town alone. Even if she had to stow away in the canoe.

The day she packed the last bag, the temperature finally crept past sixty-five degrees for the first time. Perfect baseball weather, she thought, although Matt had spent most of an idyllic afternoon scowling over survey maps and charts outside their tent. "Hey," she called, "how about taking a break to pitch me a few?"

"Mmm?"

"The ball's over by you."

"In a second."

She adjusted her stance, limbered up with her bat, waited, limbered up again, and finally stood the bat upright and leaned on the knob as a support. "Anything wrong?"

He ran one hand through his hair. "The last batch of figures is a bit off what I anticipated."

"Not as good?"

"Better. At this rate, your aunt's going to love me."

"Fantastic!" Nita abandoned her batting stance to slip her arms around his waist, rest her chin on his shoulder, and peer at his maps. They were no more comprehensible to her than the Jesuit manuscript that had brought them together, but being near him was all she needed. "Actually," she murmured, "how Aunt Addy's managed to hold out this long is a mystery to me."

"I'll feel better when I find the spout."

"We'll find it. You and I are not only going to make piles of money, we're going to make *history*."

He laughed. "You think so?"

"Trust me." She scooped up the ball lying on the ground beside him and lobbed it to him. "I bet the results from those first assays will crack out champagne in Vancouver *and* Chicago."

"I'll know tomorrow."

"I've been thinking maybe I could tag along," she said, swallowing hard in an effort to sound casual.

"Tomorrow?"

"It's about time, don't you think? All the stuff you've been bringing back makes me curious. The place must be a Mecca for shoppers. Besides, if the ore ever gives out, I could corner the rabbit market and put all the

Indian women to work. I mean, a cottage industry would be useful. Jack up the local economy. And I know some buyers at Neiman-Marcus who would kill to get their hands on blankets like—"

He cut her short. "The town isn't much to look at. I think you'd be disappointed."

"*You* seem to like it well enough."

"I've lived on a reservation. I know what to expect."

The shadowed watchfulness in his eyes proved how much accusation had crept into her voice. "Fine," she said with a strained gaiety. "You can give me a guided tour."

"You really intend to come?"

"I need a little reassurance that you're not ashamed of me."

"What are you talking about?"

"It seems like the most obvious explanation for taking such pains to make sure I never meet your friends."

"Nita, how could you imagine that was the reason?" His jaw clenched and he passed the ball from one hand to the other several times before he raised his eyes to hers. "It never occurred to me you'd feel . . ."

"The way you've felt?"

"I guess that's what I do mean," he said slowly.

"I keep telling you I'm only human."

"Come here." His voice was husky and the ball rolled onto the grass unnoticed while he held out his hand. "I'm sorry. I'm still a long way from knowing how to handle this."

"But you'll take me with you?"

He gave her a crooked grin. "Funny thing is, I always hated to leave you behind."

If going to town involved a change of pace, Nita saw immediately that Matt hadn't exaggerated the decline in atmosphere. She wrinkled her nose at the derelict motel cottages on the edge of the straggling collection of shingled buildings serving as a main street. Weathered signs identified a run-down Laundromat and a few stores. At the far end of the street a limp flag hung in front of the post office. Where Matt had found the gifts he'd brought back was as much of a mystery to her as his ability to follow an invisible trail.

Her face lit up, however, when Russell's supply drop disgorged a collection of letters. While Matt loaded their packs, she sat on the unpainted wooden steps of the post office building to read. Her sunlit halo of blond curls drew more glances here than her sleekly coiffed hair had drawn in New York. Even the white-faced hunting dogs slouching along the street seemed to stare. Although she couldn't help wondering whether the passersby knew Matt, Nita weathered this attention with professional aplomb. She raised her head only to smile at a boy of ten or eleven wearing a baseball T-shirt with the name of the reservation. Wrapped around the railing beside her, he fixed her with unblinking eyes beneath bangs cut as straight as the thin line of his mouth.

"I see you found a friend," Matt said when he came out.

"A fellow baseball fan," she said.

"His dad and I used to have a running pitching duel, didn't we, Jimmy?"

Smiling at the boy's fierce nod, Nita handed Matt two of the letters. "Aunt Addy and Libby wrote to me, but these are for you. The one you can smell from where you're standing is Cookie's. I'll bet she's asking how soon you can come to Monterey. Russell sent the other."

"Must have liked the assay reports."

"Well enough to have Holiday Mines printed on his stationery. I should have warned you to file at least one claim in your own name before you let my megalomaniacal brother into the deal." Puzzled by the sudden shadow over Matt's expression, she added, "But Libby sent the real news. Blake's doing a photo essay on the Trans-Canadian Highway. Isn't that terrific? She wants to know how to find us."

"If they fix a date, we'll meet them."

Nita glanced down at her worn jeans, wrinkled shirt, and unpolished nails, then ran both hands through hair that had taken on its natural curl with a vengeance. "She probably wouldn't recognize me now that I've gone native."

"Nobody'd mistake you for a native."

"I don't know whether to be glad or sorry." She cheerfully shouldered her pack and struggled to rise with the load. If they were going more than a hundred yards, she'd have to do the distance doubled over. "Even if I could move, it looks like sightseeing in this metropolis would take about twelve seconds. Do you spend your time paying calls or what?"

"Stay put. I'll pick you up in about an hour."

At the moment immobility seemed her only option, but letting him out of her sight wasn't in her plans. "Give me a boost and I'll come along."

"It's only a council meeting. You'd be bored."

"You sound like Russell—no female intruders." Because Matt was avoiding her eye, she added, "What council?"

He ran one hand through his hair in an unconscious gesture of discomfort. She always longed to do the same thing for the opposite reason. "Under the Department of Indian Affairs, tribal business is handled by elected representatives."

"So why are you going?"

"They're discussing mining rights."

She gaped at him. "And you thought I'd be *bored?*"

"Basically," he said, looking more uncomfortable than ever, "it'll be a philosophical discussion."

"Swell. My knowledge of Indian philosophy is restricted to how Cleveland handles its outfield and how the Redskins pick their rookies. I could use a little education."

A heroic effort and an assist from the railing made it possible for her to haul herself to her feet. Pausing to recover her breath a little before lunging forward, she turned back to the boy, whose stare had not wavered. "Are you a pitcher like your dad?"

"Like to bat."

"So do I." With a jerk of her head, she indicated Matt's departing back. "Maybe he'll let me take in a game sometime."

"He pitches at the powwow every year."

"No kidding! Then I'll probably see you there." Waving farewell, she lumbered after Matt as quickly as her load allowed. "You've been holding out on me again," she said, gasping slightly by the time she caught up with him. "This town has definite entertainment potential."

"Look, Nita, council meetings aren't open to the public."

"I was thinking about baseball. When's that powwow thing?"

"The end of August."

"Okay, I'll make you a deal. Promise we'll go and I'll skip the council meeting—do a graceful fade right after you introduce me. Now that the temperature's reached an all-time high, maybe I can eavesdrop through an open window. Just so I can tell Aunt Addy I'm keeping you honest," she added with a grin.

The six council representatives sat on folding chairs around a long table in a bare schoolroom with a wooden floor. Curtains blew limply at the windows. With their sleeves rolled up above their elbows, and their glasses, cigarettes, and wedding bands, the men might have been social workers or union members—except for the fact that all six had jet-black hair and permanent tans.

"My partner, Nita Holiday," Matt said. "This is Henry Kingbird, Vernon French, Dan Rouse, Eugene Stillday, Gordon Morrissey, and Jerry Bernaise."

A blur of names: some French—like Matt's own, she realized with a tiny shock—others Scottish or Irish. Probably they came from lineages going back to the first Canadian settlers. Except the full-bloods. They, of course, went further back.

Wondering which of them held the clue she needed, she fixed each man with what she hoped was an open and trustworthy look and held out her hand. None of their expressions altered. If her jeans had been a masquerade costume and her hair a wig, she couldn't have felt more out of place. This must have been what Matt endured when he met her relatives, she thought. Nevertheless, she struggled to find some common ground.

"I hope I'll be able to see Matt pitch at your powwow," she said.

The eldest man, whose name she remembered because Kingbird seemed so apt, gazed beyond and through her. "Powwow is dancing. For spirits, not tourists."

His response pretty well dried up her ideas for conversation, but Henry Kingbird didn't seem satisfied simply to make her feel unwelcome. "Gold makes white men crazy," he continued. "No good for Indians."

Nita's all-purpose smile wavered. "I guess that's what Matt came to talk to you about, isn't it? Well, don't let me hold up your meeting."

Sending a pleading glance in Matt's direction, she backed toward the door. By some miracle, she didn't trip over her own feet, and as soon as she was outside she dumped her pack on a spot covered with stubble that passed for grass. Through the open windows floated a singsong chant. Probably Ojibwa again, she thought—and with Matt's baritone unmistakable among the Indians' voices. Somehow not understanding a word made her feel separated from him by more than just the thickness of a shingled wall.

Well, what had she expected? Instant acceptance just because *he'd* made such a hit with *her* family? She'd had a lot less experience with Indians than he'd had with city people. And if *he* thought all Chicago people were crass, the council members probably had even stronger reasons to suspect her motives. Hopefully, his friends wouldn't be as hostile. Maybe the woman who'd woven their blanket would realize Nita had come north to follow the man who made her heart sing, not the lure of gold.

In any case, brooding wouldn't change anyone's opinion. She started to slit the monogrammed blue envelope of her aunt's letter, but sitting amid both poverty and the immensity of untouched land made Chicago seemed totally unreal, and rising voices inside the council room claimed her attention once more.

Scraps of information were all she grasped: epidemic drunkenness, poor diet, fears for the future. But even in the scraps she caught the pain of ugly preconceptions turning into truths. Picturing dark eyes refusing to meet one another across the table, she felt the hurt Matt must have known for years.

When Henry Kingbird spoke, his voice seemed to come from far away. "Mines will destroy the land."

"Dammit, Henry!" a younger voice exploded. "Minerals are our only resource. If we don't act, the whole reserve's gonna end up on welfare and the bottle. Is that what you want?"

"What are we talking about here?" someone else interrupted.

"Yeah, Matt. Show us the maps."

"There's a possibility," Matt said, "I may have to revise my calculations when I find the spout." A quiver of intensity underlay his voice, as it did whenever he had a lot at stake. "The way I see the lode shaping up, the bulk of the ore lies south and east of my camp, not west toward the reserve. That means there shouldn't be much pressure to take aboveground work near the lines, yet the quality of the ore ought to interest an existing operation in buying rights to follow their veins out underground later on. I've sketched the readings I've been getting on the survey map."

Beneath the rustle of heavy paper being unrolled, the conversation fell to an undistinguishable hum. If Matt could convince Henry Kingbird the council had panicked over nothing and that nobody was planning to dig up the town, Nita thought, the whole thing ought to blow over. Especially if the promise of a mine brought in those badly needed jobs. Certain Matt was equal to the job of stating their case without giving the Indians so much information that one of them could beat Lamartine-Holiday to the claims office, Nita returned to her aunt's letter. In her mind, Aunt Addy was more dangerous than a whole tribe of Indians.

Nita, dear—You have no idea how we worried about you when all your luggage was returned and Russell confessed he had sabotaged your sleeping bag. He kept repeating that your fate was sealed. For some reason he seemed to find this highly entertaining. I hope you are protected sufficiently from the damp without it. A stiff nightcap helps ward off the chill, so I took the liberty of suggesting Russell send you a few bottles of brandy. Do not let these fall into the hands of the local Indians as I understand the effects of drink on them are rather negative.

By now I assume you've discovered more about Matthew's past connections. Remember, dear, in business the rule is, Every man for himself. Or woman, it goes without saying. I'm sure *he* keeps this principle well in mind . . .

Suddenly, Matt's voice sharpened to a note of passionate intensity. The words he chose wrenched Nita's attention from her reading.

"Henry, the tribe can't go backward! Some of the old ways have to be left behind."

"The land is part of our body," the old man persisted, "and we are part of the land. We do not possess. How can we sell or give away?"

"The land near the power place won't be touched. You have my word."

"How can you prevent white men from digging, once the location of the gold is known?"

Another voice muttered, "Or rewriting the laws."

"Let Matt answer," the old man insisted. "We trusted him in this."

Baffled, and filled with a vague anxiety, Nita held her breath through a seemingly endless pause, but when Matt finally spoke he used the Ojibwa language. The change made her breathe in sharply and clutch her aunt's letter. As if by common consent, the conversation flowed on in words she couldn't understand. What did Matt want to discuss that she wasn't to know? she wondered. Whose side was he on? Rooted to the spot beneath the open window, she skimmed the rest of Aunt Addy's letter with new urgency.

The other day, quite by chance, your uncle spoke to a boyhood chum who teaches at Matthew's university. Naturally, since the opportunity presented itself, he made few inquiries. It seems Matthew was active in a militant Indian organization called AIM. (American Indian Movement, you know, and one may well wonder what their "aim" is.) Of course, we trust your judgment implicitly, dear, but a word to the wise, etc., etc. After all, there *is* a great deal of money involved.

You must be getting that marvelous tan one always envies in blondes. As I remember, Matthew himself seemed quite dramatically *bronzed*.

Your loving aunt,
Adele

Hardly reading to the end, Nita crumpled the paper into a ball and flung it aside. Damned insinuations! she thought. Her aunt wrote as if Matt were planning to scalp the Holiday bank balances with his trusty tomahawk. What was wrong with being committed to the mine partly because he thought it would help the Indians? There'd be more than enough to go around. Two hours spent in town would persuade *anyone* action was needed.

A breeze tumbled the crumpled blue paper over the grass. She gave chase, unwilling to risk the chance of anyone reading it—not only for Matt's sake, but because she felt ashamed. Yet, as she bent to retrieve it, still scoffing at her aunt's innuendos, her own suspicions slowly came into focus. Hadn't he warned her he had something to hide?

When the council meeting broke up, she fairly flew to Matt's side. "How'd it go?"

He crouched to inspect her pack with as much attention as if the load could have shifted during the wait. "Fine."

"I bet you convinced them prosperity was just around the corner, didn't you? Mining jobs for the masses?"

Without smiling, he looked up at her. "Tearing apart a forest isn't work for an Indian, Nita."

"But even if they didn't work in the mine," she said urgently, "having it nearby would give the town a boost. Really liven things up around here. Construction jobs, more people to be fed, gas stations, service facilities . . ."

"They realize that," he said quietly.

She swallowed. "But that's not what everyone wants?"

"No."

"And you?"

"I presented our case."

"Who gets included in 'our'? What did you tell them in there that you didn't want me to know?"

"Nita, you have to trust me about this. There's too much you don't understand."

"You bet there is! You see my aunt's letter?" She held out the crumpled blue pages in her fist. "She thinks you're playing both sides on this project. And have been all along. She knows about your Indian connections."

"I wondered how soon she'd ferret that out." He folded his hand over Nita's fist and held it. "I was involved with AIM because it was one of the few voices for Indian rights in the whole country. That may qualify me as a dangerous radical in your aunt's eyes, but it doesn't make me a crook."

"Why didn't you tell me?"

"Doesn't your aunt's attitude make that obvious?"

Her mouth trembled. "You could have trusted me."

"With everything of mine," he said, rubbing his finger back and forth over her taut knuckles. "But there are issues at stake here that aren't mine to share."

"Who I am, what I feel, doesn't count, does it? Henry Kingbird won't bother to check whether I fit his classifications; he just wants to keep me out."

"Nita, I didn't intend you two to meet on these terms."

"Even when Aunt Addy figured you were a crook, she let you make your case!"

"Wealth and power make taking chances easier."

"At least she told you where you stood."

"And Henry told you," he said quietly.

"Are you saying the best we can do is long for each other across a gulf neither of us created?"

"That depends."

"On what?"

The look he fixed on her didn't waver. "Mostly, I guess, on us."

Eight

During the next few weeks the noise of the diamond drill ate up the stillness, along with hundreds of feet of rock. The five young geese became indistinguishable from their parents, and the color of the berries Nita collected in her bark buckets changed from red to blue.

By now she and Matt had covered every subject from batting averages and which stadium served the best hot dogs to Chicago Style architecture, the peculiarities of the modeling business, and how long after he made his millions Garrison Keillor might go on chronicling life in Lake Wobegon. Since the day of the council meeting, however, Matt had avoided allusions to the gulf emerging between them the way a person might favor a tender muscle or a blistered heel. Although always gentle with her, often ending a playful moment with a caress, he walled the deepest level of his thoughts inside a reserve that hung like an autumn haze across their sunniest hours.

The look of strain that had taken possession of his face that day in town seldom disappeared completely. As they began taking samples nearer the reservation, frowning silence and not cheers of triumph greeted results far better than any they'd found before. Matt spent more and more time poring over his charts, hedged his responses to Nita's growing concern that competitors might beat them to the claims office, and pressed his search for the spout as desperately as if each assay were predicting failure instead of wild suc-

SOLID GOLD PROSPECT • 133

cess. If he were plotting as Aunt Addy suspected, Nita often thought, he wasn't enjoying his work.

"Matt, haven't we done enough for today?" she pleaded the evening before the powwow as the last glow of orange disappeared below the tree line. "It's so dark I'll have to hang onto your belt to make it back to camp."

He grinned faintly. "Could be worse.'

"You mean I could be leading?"

"We'd probably end up in Toronto."

She looked up from her struggle to snap a pickax and an army shovel onto her pack in the failing light. "Hey, we could stay in our old suite. You owe me some champagne."

"I'd give a lot to take this project further back in time than Toronto."

"But we've almost finished the hard part! Filing the claims can't be much more complicated than bringing our results into the Thunder Bay office and watching their eyes bug out."

Shrugging into his pack, he shook his head. "It's not the work; it's the whole idea. If you asked me today whether finding gold here will turn out to be the best or the worst thing I ever did, I couldn't tell you."

Surprise twisted her around so quickly she lost her balance. Chunks of stone from a pile of tailings dug into her palm. "How can you say that?"

"It's the truth."

"But three months ago the mine meant everything to you. Not just the money, but proving you were right, even helping to build up an industry here."

"I'm starting to realize a man can change his whole life—and maybe more lives than his own—by simply signing his name to a piece of paper. Holiday Mines may make you and your family and a bunch of speculators out in Vancouver richer than you already are, but no amount of money can put a wilderness back together once it's been raped by a mining operation."

"That sounds like what Henry Kingbird was saying at the meeting," she said slowly. "Was he the one who changed your mind?"

"A lot of contradictions I've pushed aside for years

are coming to a head this summer. When my brother and I were growing up we learned to live in the bush for months without leaving a single mark, but I'm an engineer because I never forgot my father's pride in building locks and dams that could transform whole areas almost beyond recognition. I suppose I've wanted to reconcile those two points of view all my life—even though I knew that's what had torn my parents apart. Until this summer mining seemed to be the answer. I was onto something big enough to qualify for the American dream in Technicolor and I spent three months a year in the field, touching base with the other side."

"But you've changed your mind since the council."

"Yup." He gave her a wan smile. "The samples are playing hell with my estimates."

"Nobody's going to blame you for finding a bigger strike than you planned! Russell's gold-embossed letterhead didn't look as though he was *disappointed*."

"Nothing's guaranteed until I find the spout."

"Can't we file without it?"

"Yes." He looked at her fixedly. "People have been known to file without it."

"Then it doesn't matter. It won't be the end of the world if we don't find ours."

His jaw tightened. "I wish I thought you were right."

Although Russell had scrambled the labels on the food he sent in the supply drop, the contents of the foil packages proved edible. Surprise added a certain zest to their evening meals. "Lobster Newburg?" Matt asked, inspecting the main course as Nita stirred the pot suspended over the fire.

"We should be so lucky."

She ladled the pale substance into their dishes. "Whatever it is, I'm going to love it. Nothing like crushing rock to give a person an appetite." Her expression changed with the first spoonful. "This is definitely not lobster Newburg."

"Creamed chicken?"

"Guess again."

Tasting generously, Matt sputtered over the contents of his spoon. "Tapioca pudding!"

"Russell knows I've hated it ever since I was a kid."

"Lots of milk and eggs."

"Ugh." Nita was too hungry not to eat, but when she got up on her knees to toss their empty birchbark bowls on the fire she muttered. "Wait till I get my hands on that Russell."

"Don't be too hard on him."

"He deserves the worst—ninety days of vouchers at the Chatterbox Café. Daily doses of Tomato–Ginger-Ale Aspic and Stewed Prune Surprise."

Matt laughed. "I have a soft spot for your brother."

"Why?"

"He thought of us as a team before I believed it myself."

Firelight added glitter to the look Matt fixed on her, and a familiar sense of longing tightened its fist around Nita's heart. But she was beginning to suspect passion lacked the irresistible force of gravity. Even nights that swept her doubts beyond the far reaches of oblivion wouldn't necessarily keep their lives from flying in opposite directions. "I'm not sure you believe we're a team yet," she said without looking at him. "In some ways, making love hasn't . . . hasn't brought us any closer."

"Nita, don't say that."

She raised her head. "There's so much we can't talk about. Simple, ordinary things people in love ought to share without thinking. You scarcely mention your brother or your mother. You've never really explained why you're so committed to this place. Often when I watch your face in the firelight, no matter how hard I try, I can't imagine what you're thinking. The fact that I'm an outsider stands between us, yet you've only taught me how to deal with the woods, never with the people who live here. Don't you understand, Matt? Sometimes I'm afraid that by the time you learn to be open with me, I'll—I'll have forgotten how to trust you."

For several minutes he didn't speak. The embers glowed as though the intensity of his look were forcing them to burn. "I know what you're saying. I should be asking you to share not only my bed, but my life. That's what I want. Or what I would want if I could tell you the facts you deserved to know from the beginning."

"Then *tell* me!"

"My situation is so damned tangled now." His hand sketched a gesture combining impatience with despair. "I don't see how I'll get free without doing somebody some harm."

"If you'd explain, I could try to help."

"You shouldn't have to shoulder my problems."

"But how can we be a team if you shut me out? We don't need any phony barriers between us."

"They're real enough," he said grimly.

"Not to me."

"Only because I can't face showing them to you."

"Isn't it time?"

"It may be too late."

"Matt . . ."

"I love you. That's the one clear thing in all this mess. And every day I wonder how long I'll be able to keep you."

As if to deny his fears, he reached out to draw her close. They clung to each other in the circle of dying light, the fierce pressure of his arms his only admission of the burden he refused to let her share.

That night Nita dreamed she was riding up and down in a glass elevator in Russell's gigantic new hotel, lugging shoulder bags bulging with gold and desperately trying to ransom Matt from a conspiracy involving the Chicago Mafia, famous players from old Cubs' teams, and Hollywood Indians. When she finally managed to deliver the gold in a shower that sent them all scrambling while she and Matt floated to freedom beneath a parachute of rabbit fur, she awoke and took the dream's happy ending as sign. If romance heroines took their fate into their own hands, why shouldn't she? Today could be her day.

Everything pointed in that direction: brilliant sunshine, a flawless blue sky, baseball in the offing, and Indians—presumably at their most amiable and relaxed —to wow if not to pow. From his perch atop a rock, surrounded by young geese who'd grown as tame as pets, Matt watched her spin through her share of the chores like a teen on prom day. "When are we leaving?" she asked every fifteen minutes.

"Soon."

"What time does it start?"

"When people get there," he said, laughing as her eyes widened. "That's Indian time: eating, working, or doing whatever you have in mind when it feels right."

"Well, your inner clock must be slow," she exclaimed. "The time has felt right to me for about two hours."

"Eager to get your hands on a ball?"

"Hey! You mean I can play?"

"Softball, maybe."

"Softball! That's a girl's game."

He snaked out his arm to encircle her waist, pull her close, and nuzzle the silk T-shirt that fitted her like a colored skin. "In that outfit, nobody could mistake you for anything else."

"Fine talk." She luxuriated for a moment in his embrace, then reared back and planted a finger in the middle of his chest. "But you've seen me bat. So you better make sure I'm not playing for the other side."

"I'd have to strike you out."

"Just you try."

Lifting her shirt, he tickled her bare midriff with kisses. "That's not what I feel like doing right now."

"It'll be dark before we get there. Don't you have a game to pitch? Or do they have night games in the Indian league?"

"Nope. Dancing."

"I suppose you'll turn out to be the star!"

"Wait till you see me done up in feathers."

Suddenly wistful, picturing herself excluded among a circle of watchers while he danced, she tugged his hair with one hand to halt his kisses. "Don't tease me, Matt."

"I wasn't."

"What do you mean?"

He smiled, but the too familiar wary look was back. "Tribal traditions were as important to my mother as they are to Henry Kingbird. She believed the Ojibwa couldn't survive without them and spent a tremendous amount of energy on keeping them alive. She taught me as much as I had patience to learn."

"Knowing she was marking you forever?"

"I think she hoped someday I'd care as much as she did."

His face told her how much it had cost him to cut even this tiny door in the wall between them. The moment wasn't one for bells and whistles—not the dizzying communion their bodies knew—but even as Nita smiled at him, her eyes stung. Maybe this would be their day as well as hers.

"Will you teach me?" she asked gently.

"The dance steps?"

"Everything."

"I'm not an expert." He hesitated. "A lot of Indians don't really know what being Indian means."

"As much as you can, then. Please, Matt. I don't expect an instant how-to. Three months ago I'd never laid eyes on an Ojibwa, had no idea a couple of hundred Indians were scraping together a living here in the middle of nowhere, much less that someday I'd feel partly responsible for their future. But now, even if *you* didn't care so much, I couldn't forget what I've seen and heard. It's crazy how things turn out, isn't it? I always figured I'd end up with a baseball fan. He was going to be so tickled because I practically learned to read from the sports pages and wanted to watch every game. But I didn't bargain on not being able to be happy until I learned to walk in the mental shoes of total strangers. And not even shoes, *moccasins!*"

"You won't like what you hear."

"I'll handle it somehow. I don't want my ignorance to keep us apart."

The joint rhythm of their paddles sent the canoe up

the lake in the direction of town with a sleek, easy movement. Scarcely aware of her activity, Nita bent her attention to what Matt was saying as though their future could be assured if she memorized every word.

"Fifty or sixty years ago," he began, "the Indians around here still lived pretty much in the old ways. Families had their own areas where they trapped during the winter. About May they'd come down to plant their gardens and some would work as guides and cabin girls at the fishing camps. On Treaty Day, the Indian agent paid a certain sum to the head of every family and they held a big powwow. After blueberrying in August, they'd start to harvest their gardens and sell dried berries to buy winter supplies. In September they'd rice."

"Rice?"

"Gather wild rice. When the harvest was in there'd be another big powwow, then deer and moose hunting, and by October they'd be back on the trapline for the winter. Each season supplied its own kind of food. Unless they went to the missionaries' big Christmas feast, families spent the winter alone, but summer was sociable. Work mixed with play. Tribal taboos and Indian agents' sanctions weren't in conflict."

"If it was such a great life, what went wrong?"

"You'd probably get as many answers to that one as there are Indians. Nobody's life is the same now as it was fifty years ago, but for the Indians, the changes turned out to be catastrophic. For example, the government would make a proposal that looked all right on the surface, like expanding medical services. Sounds good, right? But while the government agents were putting those wonderful social programs in place, the whole cultural structure was going down like a row of dominoes."

"That doesn't make sense."

"Because you don't think like an Indian. And the tribes didn't see what was coming because they couldn't think like businessmen or bureaucrats. For the government, stabilizing a tribe near a highway made providing schools and services more efficient. So they took people who flourished on space and an intimate connection to their land and clustered them into tight, artificial little communities. The move took away easy access to the Indians' livelihood, and water pollution cut into the fishing, so the government replaced what it had taken with welfare. Then they educated away any self-respect the people had left."

"And it's too late to change?"

"It is if they did it because they wanted the use of the land. And that's what most Indians believe."

"They don't know that for a fact!"

"Even if it wasn't the reason, the effect's the same. Suspicion makes people just as bitter as truth. It's only in fiction that right and wrong show up so clearly that characters don't spend their whole adult lives wondering what the hell is going wrong."

For what seemed a long time he paddled in silence. From the town the schizophrenic sound of drumbeats and racing motorcycles drifted across the water.

"Matt, you don't have to solve the world's problems."

"I can't even solve my own. Look, I'm not asking you to believe what I'm going to tell you next, but I believe it. Do you know anything about Indian rock paintings?"

She shook her head.

"They mark spots—a clump of trees, a group of rocks— where Indians believe the land exerts a special force. People talk about a place that's been ill-used sending out bad vibrations. Well, for those who can see it, good land sends out a kind of light. Places with that power lay a hand on anyone who visits them. It's a feeling you don't forget, like coming close to the answer of what life and death are all about."

With sudden clarity, she remembered one of the remarks she'd overheard at the meeting. "One of those places is on the reservation."

"Yes."

"You've been there?"

"Many times."

Her paddle paused in midair, and the canoe swung in a large circle. "And you promised to keep it safe," she said slowly.

"I thought I could."

"But now you're not so sure?"

"The richest part of the lode may lie too close."

"So people—white people—will want to dig there."

"With the results we're getting? I'll say they will."

She swallowed. If the spout turned up under or even near a sacred site, a confrontation between the interests of Holiday Mines and Indian beliefs would be inevitable. With Matt in the middle—unless he went over to the Indians' side and left *her* in the middle.

"What do you plan to do?" she asked.

"A couple of weeks ago I thought I knew. Now I have my hands full trying to figure out a way to keep your aunt from turning into a prophet."

Nita's heart sank, but as their canoe slid over the pebble-lined shallows, she refused to let grotesque calamities like finding too much gold in the wrong places distract her. She could worry about the mine tomorrow. The way things were going, today might be her only chance to show Matt's friends that at least one Holiday was on their side.

Her first impression of the crowd put her at ease. In matters of dress, anything went at a powwow. Just as in Chicago or New York. Thick woolly pants held up by broad gray suspenders were in, along with printed cotton dresses ordered thirty years ago from Eaton catalogs, and designer jeans like her own. So were sumptuously embroidered velveteen vests and fur trims. Feathered cowboy hats communed with headbands beaded in floral designs—both accessorized with heavy dark-rimmed glasses and digital watches. A sprinkling of baseball shirts foretold the game to come.

"Reminds me of a country fair," she said to Matt. "Are your friends here yet?"

"They're pretty much all friends."

"You're kidding," Nita exclaimed with a stab of consternation. Charming one or two people might be within the realm of possibility. Becoming a public heroine was stretching it. "At least *some* of these people must be tourists. What about the fellow lounging against the shack with the antlers over the door?"

Matt shifted his concentration from a knot of teens gathered around parked cycles. "That's Jimmy's dad, Ken."

She blew out her breath. "I'll bet there's every kind of Indian here except one with blue eyes."

"There are some."

"No wonder they have identity crises. Well, they say sports is the big entrée for minorities. Maybe I'd better tackle your pitcher friend first."

"You just mixed a metaphor."

"If I'd mixed my blood," she grumbled, "I bet I could play."

Matt looked at her strangely, but allowed her to lead the way past a drummer whose equipment, complete with padded, feather-decorated drumsticks, would have sent a rock band into ecstasies, a toddler wildly swinging a minuscule plastic bat at an imaginary ball. A baby dangled peacefully from the branch of a tree in a cradle made of a folded blanket, and a woman as seamed and weathered as a figurehead from an old sailing vessel swigged canned soda as she stirred a steaming pot over an open fire.

"Where've you been all summer, Lamartine?" the drummer called. "Haven't seen you around."

"Some days he's an Indian, some not," the old woman muttered. Matt grinned at her and countered with a question in Ojibwa. A monosyllabic answer, accompanied by a jerk of her head in the direction of the main street, didn't interrupt the woman's unblinking scrutiny of Nita's hair. Before she started twisting her braids like a schoolgirl, Nita leaned over to savor the steaming liquid.

"I bet Matt wishes I could get smells like this from *our* pot," she said.

"Wild rice soup." With a dented ladle the old woman filled a cup for her. "Make him teach you."

Nita smiled. The future tense promised status. When Matt introduced the woman as the maker of their blanket, Nita's face lit up even more. Juggling her spoon and cup, she held out her hand to clasp the gnarled brown one. For a few minutes she forgot baseball in an enthusiastic discussion of the commercial opportunities available through Neiman-Marcus catalogs, Hudson Bay stores, sales reps, and commission percentages.

"Whad'ya say, Matt!" Jimmy's dad hollered. At closer range, his resemblance to the boy on the post office steps was unmistakable: the same broad, almost Oriental features, the same thin mouth. In a few more years, Nita thought, his son would be swaggering through a powwow crowd, an open can of soda in his hand, his childish stare grown as wary as his father's, whose gaze flicked around her without meeting her eye. "Thought your arm would be too out of shape to play," Ken said.

"Don't count on it," Matt answered. "Your team all set?"

"More or less."

"If your infield's thin," Nita said, "I'm itching to play."

"Don't need any softball players."

She bit back a pungent answer. Even feeling lucky, she couldn't afford to push too hard. "Well, can I watch you guys warm up?"

"Got her scouting us, Matt?" Ken asked.

"Nope. Just brought her along to learn a little 'injunuity.' " He smiled as he took her hand and called what must have been a parting message in Ojibwa to the old woman.

Nita slid onto the players' bench beside Jimmy. The boy looked as frustrated as she felt, and she gave him a sympathetic smile. "Hi. Mind if I grab some bench?" The boy shook his head.

Although play hadn't started, the familiar magic of the game took hold the moment Nita gazed out onto the field. As long as the sun was up she wouldn't spare a thought to her problems from the first windup until the last pitch crossed the plate. Baseball and romances might not work in the same way, but they both worked.

Watching Matt throw made her doubly happy. Setting aside her flagrant bias on his behalf, she loved the pure, elegant efficiency of his movements. Who needed showy mannerisms? Two speeds on his curve and his fastball, a knuckler, and control over the strike zone would do it all. From personal experience she knew he had good hands. And she'd learned from his victories over Uncle Bo that he was also a tactician. The way he seemed to scan the crowd every time he wound up would have caught Aunt Addy's eye as proof of his natural aptitude for a pitcher's real strength—deceit.

With an effort she shifted her attention to his opponents. "Who's your best batter?" she asked Jimmy.

"My dad."

"Hey, a pitcher who can hit. That's pretty rare."

Her praise made the boy's eyes flicker in her direction with a look bordering on comradeship. "Old Pizza Face over there thinks he's hot."

She judged he wasn't a favorite. "The guy who looks as though his face caught fire and somebody put it out with a track shoe?"

"Yeah." Jimmy grinned. "That's him."

Together they analyzed the batters as they stepped up to the plate and hunkered down. No problem for Pizza Face to look mean, but tension lessened his control. He mowed his bat into the first pitch and missed.

"Good back-to-front swing," Nita pronounced judicially, "but he doesn't know how to wait. That's why your dad's a better hitter even though he doesn't have much power."

As the practice broke off in preparation for the first inning, she scooped up a few balls. "Grab a bat," she said to Jimmy. "I'll show you." A few minutes later Jimmy's father came over to wipe his face on a scrap of old T-shirt substituting for a towel.

"Learning something?" he asked his son.

"She says I'm a knee-knocker 'n if I stand like this . . ." Before swinging at Nita's next pitch, Jimmy demonstrated the slight alteration in foot posture she had suggested. She threw the ball and he drove it out between the second baseman's legs. Instant confusion among Matt's outfielders. Gratified surprise on Jimmy's face. And in his father's expression Nita read a reluctant admission that she might know something about baseball after all.

For five innings the game seesawed back and forth

as a pitchers' duel. A run on each side pepped up the sixth. When the first baseman on Ken's team sprained his ankle, Nita thought her luck had come in, but Jimmy's dad didn't offer her the spot. She couldn't decide what counted against her most, being white or being female.

"Have an idea out there!" she yelled in exasperation as Matt's butterfingered outfield let a weak line drive turn into a tweener worth a second score. With teammates who couldn't catch a ball any better than a bunch of old ladies, why couldn't he trust her to play? she wondered.

When the score evened out again in the eighth, Matt began to patrol the crowd while he waited for his turn at bat, but he denied her accusation of weakening nerves. "If we pull ahead, I might persuade the guys to let you into the last inning," he said.

"Out of bravado?"

"Nope. Pity."

She was too eager to turn down any terms. "How far ahead?"

He grinned. "Say fifteen or sixteen."

"Oh, get lost," she said, throwing a spare mitt at him. "If I were playing with the opposition, we'd walk all over you!"

By the end of the ninth, with two outs for Ken's team and the first baseman hobbled by his swollen ankle, her patience wore out. "Let me go in for your first base," she pleaded with Ken. "What have you got to lose? Even if he hit, he couldn't run."

"You think you could take Lamartine over the wall?"

"I could try."

"Nobody else can."

"Nobody else knows him so well!"

He nodded. "All right."

Giving Jimmy a thumbs-up sign, she grabbed a bat and ran to take her stance at the plate. Pizza Face gestured angrily, but she turned her sole focus on the pitcher's mound.

Even for Matt, she knew a woman with a bat in her hand was bound to be a woman first and a batter second. He'd hold back his fastball for fear of hurting her. If she snugged a bit closer to the plate, she might force him to lay the ball outside, where she could put the head of her bat full on it. Scuffing her feet, she adjusted her stance a little and prepared to wait.

A high slider, spinning so hard it looked like a red dot, slammed toward her. She held an instant before she let fly. Foul. But nobody else had touched Matt's slider all afternoon, and a general murmur of amazement gave her satisfaction. In a calculated gamble, sure he'd hate to see her go down in ignominious defeat, she let a pair of tricky curveballs go by for strikes. Let him think curves weren't her thing.

"Come on, Blondie!" someone called from the crowd.

She shook the tension from her shoulders. The next pitch was all or nothing. Nothing, if she'd misjudged him. But when the ball came it was another curve, medium slow this time and sweet as butter. Just the pitch she wanted.

"Sorry, love," she muttered, opening up to connect with a satisfying whack.

The ball took off down the field like a floating rope. She was pumping for second when the crowd's roar told her Matt's outfield had let him down again. Home free with the winning run in her pocket! Well, he couldn't say she hadn't warned him.

He put his arm around her shoulder as the players jogged off the field. "Should have taken your advice," he said.

"You didn't just give me that hit, did you?"

"Nope. You faked me out."

"I wouldn't have," she said, nestling against him with a little purr of satisfaction, "if you'd get it through your head that I mean what I say."

"Take you on again next year," Ken called to them. "And I can always use a decent man on first."

Matt hugged her closer. "Next year I'm not loaning her out.'

A couple of players paused to congratulate her on her play. Jimmy took time out from a venison burger and fried bread garnished with blueberry jam to show off his new batting stance like a PR man. Not exactly instant popularity or universal acclaim, Nita thought, but she felt a flush of achievement. Lamartine-Holiday would make a dynamite ball team. Among other things.

The mood of the crowd intensified as the light faded, and the drums throbbed like a hectic pulse. Gathered in untidy, constantly changing clusters, people stuffed themselves with tempting food and drink. Matt didn't stop to eat, though, but pulled Nita along as though he were racing against his invisible clock.

"What's the rush?" she asked, laughing. "I thought we were on Indian time."

"There's someone you have to meet."

"Hey, Lamartine," a voice called. "Dancing's starting."

"Dancing?" She pulled up short. "I thought you were joking about being a dancer."

"No." His grip crushed her hand. "Look. Wait for me."

"Why can't I—"

"I'll be back as soon as I can."

She lost sight of him in the crowd. Where had he gone in such a hurry? she wondered. Where were any of the faces she knew? She was surrounded by strangers, all pushing forward now in the direction of the drumming and a circle of lights. She came up against a slatted fence before she realized it was there, or that the powwow ceremony had begun on the other side.

Here the drum was all-powerful, insistent, commanding. Costumed older men and women moved in the circular patterns of the dance. Among them, male dancers dressed in feathered bustles and deer-hair headdresses touched the ground lightly twice between each beat.

She began to recognize faces. Henry Kingbird, wearing dignity like an invisible robe, was the emcee. Among the dancers she spotted other men from the council and some from the baseball teams. And then she saw Matt—unmistakable in his grace, his striking features, and the bronzed body whose every lineament she knew by touch as well as sight. She twined her fingers around the slats to hold her place as bodies pressed and shoved against her.

"Matt!" she called.

"You're the blonde who's shacking up with him, aren't you?"

Nita's head snapped toward the sound of a feminine voice. Dressed in a costume jingling with hundreds of tiny metal cones, her chin held high as any princess's, the girl who had spoken was so lovely that Arlene Harrison would have shed tears of joy and gratitude and offered a contract the minute she caught sight of her. The girl's face, however, wore an expression Nita didn't have to be an Indian to understand.

"I . . . I beg your pardon?" she asked.

"Shacking up with my uncle," the girl said. "You're the reason he's hardly been around all summer."

"Your uncle . . . ?"

Unable to finish her question, Nita gazed helplessly at the pure cut of the girl's mouth, the heavily lined eyes which shared Matt's brilliance, if not his humor, and her moth-wing version of his masculine brows.

"I don't . . . I don't think I understand."

The girl shrugged and tossed her head. Earrings glinted and jingled behind the shoulder-length fall of her hair. "I guess he never told you about us."

"Us?" The realization that Matt had family living only miles from their camp cramped Nita's heart with a pain sharper than any she'd ever felt in her legs. "No, he didn't."

"Well, he told *us* about you. And your money."

Scorn vibrated in the girl's voice. So much hostility couldn't be a fabrication, Nita thought. Was "shacking up" Matt's term or his niece's deliberate cruelty? Could that be how he really saw their summer together? He'd hidden so much, perhaps it was. Struggling against her shock, Nita raised the back of her hand to her mouth. "I have to . . . have to talk to Matt."

"No use calling him to come out to you."

"Why?"

"Fancy dancers are special."

Scarcely able to concentrate on the girl's answer,

Nita sought him among the moving figures. "I know what you thought," the girl persisted. "You figured if a red man lived like a white, he wasn't an Indian at all. You thought he'd help you get our land, but he was way too smart for you."

"I'm not after your land," Nita said.

Even from a distance she felt the pang of recognition when Matt's glance met hers, the moment's pause—his body tight as a drawn bow—before the beat claimed him again.

"You're afraid now, aren't you?" the girl continued relentlessly. "It's written all over your face. You whites are always afraid a red man will cheat you if he gets the chance, the way you cheat each other."

Nita's hands felt like ice. "The same hair and skin color doesn't make people the same inside."

"No?" The metal cones on the girl's dress jangled as she flung herself away to join the dancers on the other side of the barricade. "Well, you'll find out," she called back. "Matt's one of us. And there's nothing you can do about it—not with all your money!"

Nine

Matt found her sitting on the ground beside the canoe. Still breathing hard, he crouched in the darkness beside her. "Nita, I'm sorry. I don't know what Kenora said, but—"

"She said she doesn't want me here. That I don't belong."

He groaned. "I should have told you about her."

"It doesn't matter now."

"Don't say that!"

She jerked her arm away from his hand. "What should I say? Everything's okay? It doesn't bother me that you kept our relationship in a separate compartment from the rest of your life? It doesn't matter that you didn't trust me enough to even *tell* me about your niece and I don't know what else? Why should I mind your making what we have together into something—something so second class?"

"It could never be that."

"No? Then level with me. Who's more important to you, them or me?"

"I know I can't justify what happened tonight, but will you let me explain? Kenora's my half-brother's daughter. Her mother's been in and out of alcohol abuse programs for years. When my brother died the summer after he got back from Vietnam, I more or less brought her up."

Nita swallowed hard. "And because I'm white and, as she put it, 'shacking up' with you, I get to stand in for the villain?"

"Don't blame her. I'm the one who's responsible for hurting you both. Kenora's simply fighting change in the only way she knows. I've been the one stable factor in her life. The situation around here can't give her the kind of easy acceptance or open outlook on life you take for granted. I was hoping that with enough time she'd be able to come to terms with our relationship before you met."

"Yet you told her. And you didn't tell me."

"I wasn't afraid of losing her!"

"You say you care about me, but you don't listen. I need to trust you, to be trusted."

"Nita, take a good look at me," he said harshly. "I'm more at home in what I'm wearing now than in your brother's tuxedo. Were you ready to marry an Indian?"

"Is that your answer to my question?"

"About who's more important? I don't know. I don't know if there is an answer anymore." Starlight shadowed the taut planes of his face as he stared out over the lake. "This place is in my blood. Part of me will always be tied here by memories, responsibilities, gut instincts, beliefs. Yet another part of me is as much an outsider as you are."

"Your niece claims that part's a sham."

"My life changed when I fell in love with you. That's not easy for someone else to understand."

"But, Matt, don't you see? If you can't decide where you belong, I don't fit in either. Somehow we've managed to pull each other out of place. I'm not the same ex-model from Chicago who only thought about Indians if she saw them in the movies. I see the whole world differently because of you. Wherever I go now, this place will be part of who I am, the same as you are."

Even in the darkness she felt the intensity of the look he turned on her. "If you mean that, will you—can you—give me one more chance?"

"I don't know," she said helplessly.

"Your family has a lot invested in this mine. I never imagined I'd be grateful for the contract I signed in your brother's office, but if you can't stay for me, would you stay for them?"

"You mean . . . as a partner?"

"Stay. Please. On whatever terms you need."

She stood up awkwardly, brushing at the seat of her pants while she tried to steady her voice. "I suppose it's only fair for me to stick it out until we file the claims. I wouldn't let you leave because it hurt. But you'd better ask one of your friends to lend you a tent and a sleeping bag."

Four days later Nita sat with her knees drawn up under her chin, jabbing at the fire with a stick. Underneath the coals, fish were baking inside packets of clay, but gourmet dining in honor of Blake and Libby's introduction to life in the wild couldn't be further from her thoughts. "So there he sat," she said, "looking like he just walked off the cover of a Western, and I asked, 'Who's more important to you, them or me?' "

Libby shook her head. "You haven't changed so much."

"Why beat around the bush?"

"How could he answer a question like that?"

"What's so complicated? He loves me or he doesn't. And don't start making excuses for him. In my first heart-to-heart female talk in almost four months, do you have to take *his* side?"

"Isn't that what you want?"

Their eyes met and held, then Nita swallowed and turned back to the fire. "I don't mean to jump on you. I just can't figure out how to handle this. First I find out he's the star fancy dancer at the powwow. Okay, if I were putting on an affair, I'd make him the star too. Then it turns out his half-brother drowned himself by sinking his car in a lake, leaving Matt to support little Miss Indian America. Swell. Well, not exactly *swell*, but who's your most broad-minded friend? Me, right? So I'm proud of him and I see why his commitment to this place goes a whole lot deeper than I thought. I accept the fact that he'll always be involved with what happens to this place and the people here, and that he's the one who has to decide how much involvement that will be. Logically, there's no problem."

"How about emotionally?"

"Emotionally, I feel like I ate a package of razor blades. No matter how I look at it, he trusted them when he didn't trust me. That's what hurts."

Libby put an arm across Nita's tensed shoulders. "It's okay. Cry if you want."

"Dammit! I am *not* going to cry."

Libby fished a tissue out of the pocket of her ample flannel shirt and handed it to her. "Here."

"Thanks." Nita blew her nose noisily. "I used the last of mine up yesterday. I'd sneak off into the woods, bawl, and then have to practice smiling like a toothpaste ad again. My upper lip will never be the same. And do you know what's really ironic? Matt can't even belong to the tribe! You have to be at least a quarter-breed to qualify and that's all his mother was. I told him he had just enough Indian blood to make him irresistible."

"What did he say to that?"

"He didn't even smile."

Frowning, Libby passed her another tissue. "Obviously, his background is a bigger problem for him than for you."

"Not if it splits us up, it isn't. In the beginning I diagnosed the chip on his shoulder as status anxiety. Deprived childhood or something. I thought that as soon as we found the gold my family would welcome him with greedy, open arms and, presto, no problem. Talk about oversimplification!"

"Did he ever"—Libby hesitated—"try to tell you the truth?"

"He never *lied* to me," Nita said quickly.

"But you told me he—"

"Omitted."

"Pretty drastic omissions."

Nita felt her color rise. "Now wait a minute. I thought you were arguing his side."

Sighing, Libby took off her glasses and polished them

on the tail of her shirt. Without them her face glowed rosily in spite of her concerned expression. "What I'm going to say may be futile, but somebody has to bring this up. In every other way Matt Lamartine might be the greatest guy in the world. And maybe you can accept whatever he does because of the way you feel about him. But if he can't be open with you—if you can't *trust* him to be open—what kind of future will the two of you have together?"

For a long time Nita didn't answer. White granules began to shred off the wad of damp tissue she was rolling between her hands. "You're batting one thousand on the question. Care to try for the answer?"

"You're the one who has to answer."

"What could be left to tell me? I asked him outright whether he was a bigamist, a bisexual, a child abuser, or a mass murderer."

"I take it he said no?"

"Of course he said no! I may have fallen for a romantic, idealistic, ex-radical Indian, but even I have to draw the line somewhere!"

Libby laughed. "So you're still in love."

"Look, I'm sitting here in moccasins. The geese could use my hair as a nest for another round of eggs. While any normal person would be watching TV, I'm learning to play a mouth-bow. Instead of buying a pot at Bloomingdale's, I'm baking fish in clay I dug myself. This morning—despite the fact that the temperature hasn't gone higher than seventy all summer—I washed my entire goosefleshed body in cold water. And you need to ask if I'm in *love*?" Nita looked out at the yellowing birches and her sarcasm fell away to a whisper. "If I lost him, my life would be over."

"Well," Libby said gently, "you haven't lost him. It's obvious from the vibrations between you that separate tents weren't *his* idea."

Nita nipped a quivering lip between her teeth, sniffled, and swabbed her nose again. "Passion might have been a terrific distraction, but it was never the answer to how we were going to make a life together." She demolished the tissue with ripping motions. "A life together! Would you believe I'm so mixed up that this morning when I noticed the poison ivy starting to turn, I thought, how beautiful to have an orange flag signaling the change of the seasons. Poison ivy! Six months ago, if anyone had told me I'd be waxing poetic over obnoxious weeds, I would have told them to see an analyst."

"I know Blake will take pictures until he runs out of film," Libby said placidly, leaning back on her elbows with her hands crossed high over her stomach. "For me it's the quiet that's so incredible. I can understand how easy it would be to love this place."

"In five years Blake's photographs will be historical novelties. Matt's worried because the strike's bigger than he expected. That means the scale of the change here will be bigger too. Even if we stopped taking samples tomorrow, paid back the grubstake, and disappeared, someone else would come. The word's out and rumors of gold are harder to stuff back than genies into lamps. So now, on top of everything else, I lose sleep over a kid who lives in a shack with three unmatched chairs and a store calendar on the wall over the wood box. Does it depend on me whether he ends up working for a mining company, playing ball in Minneapolis, or sinking *his* car in a lake? I even worry about Miss Indian America. Should I send her picture to Harrison and set her up to make two hundred thousand dollars a year before she's eighteen, or should I turn into another Aunt Addy, screening her beaux and making sure none of them are after her uncle's millions?"

Libby smiled at her. "You sound committed."

"Do I?"

"Isn't that at least part of the answer?"

Nita picked bits of white out of the grass around her without speaking. "So you think I should forgive him and start beading my moccasins? Assuming someday he'll be free enough of his hang-ups to propose."

"Remember how you were always comparing Blake and me to characters in your romances? Well, something tells me you haven't reached Chapter Ten of yours yet."

"You mean, the point at which the mine makes a trillion dollars, Matt buys me a horse of my own . . ."

"You start a boutique to merchandise fabulous fur blankets and a foundation for Native American artists . . ."

"I find out we're going to have triplets, Aunt Addy decides to adopt Miss Indian America, and Russell sponsors a ball club just for Indians."

"I think you've got it."

They laughed. "The only problem," Nita said, growing somber again, "is that *your* romance was a textbook case. It followed all the rules. With my luck I could be in Chapter Nine with the catastrophe yet to come."

Libby sat up. "Don't be ridiculous. There's no real problem about your family accepting Matt, is there?"

"They all think he's marvelous, except for Aunt Addy. From the beginning she sized him up as a shyster and an Indian sympathizer. As long as the claims get filed, I think she might settle for being half right."

"And there's no problem about the claims?"

"As far as my family goes, we're all set. There's gold enough for everybody. But sometimes I wonder if the damn mine won't be the last straw."

"Untold wealth. How tragic."

"Money isn't everything," Nita grumbled.

"True. Right now, a spot of dinner would be welcome. When do you think our men'll be back?"

"When it gets too dark for Blake to take pictures?"

"In that case, better trot out the hors d'oeuvres. I'm ready to gnash on roots and berries."

Surveying her friend critically for the first time, Nita said, "Unless that's all flannel under there, you might want to hold back a little."

"Actually . . . it's not flannel."

As Libby smoothed the fabric over her rounded front with a satisfied smile, Nita's mouth fell open. Then she leaped up to smother her friend in an enormous hug. "I should have guessed! Blake practically helped you across every pine needle."

"This is already the world's most-photographed baby."

"Has it ever occurred to you that you lead a charmed life?"

"Mmm. You bullied me into it."

Nita laughed. "Well, just make sure you return the favor."

The Faulkners' departure coincided with the first frost. Nita's lonely tent grew colder and she knew, as clearly as if he still lay beside her, Matt's thoughts took the same paths as hers during the long hours of the night. Often when she raised her head from a task, she caught his gaze fixed on her as though she were one of autumn's translucent yellow leaves that the next gust of wind might strip from his side and whirl away. She smiled back, clinging to her twig of hope with all her strength.

Although his need to find the spout drove him like a demon, he repeatedly postponed the date for filing the claims they'd staked. But the weather normally closed down Ontario's prospecting season in October, and his fall semester classes in Houghton would start soon. Time was running out. Every morning a fresh film of white over the grass reminded Nita that the days of their partnership were numbered.

Uncertainty about their future doubled the pressure she felt. If he couldn't commit himself, if he couldn't ask for her, all her willingness to forgive would be in vain. Sometimes, while Matt was checking survey points with increasingly obsessive care, she wandered off alone simply to escape the intensity with which she yearned for him.

"Where are you going?" he'd say the instant she moved.

"Nowhere."

"Don't get lost."

"You'd have to come after me."

"I'd come."

The day she found the stump half hidden by a growth of underbrush, she stared at it in amazement. Someone had cleanly and deliberately squared it with an ax. She had been heedless, as always, of which direction they had taken that morning, knowing only that she and Matt were staking the corners of their claims with four-foot posts. But a squared stump would be just as legal. "Matt," she cried, "have we been here before?"

"Nope."

"Not even to take samples?"

"Too near the reservation line."

"But that doesn't mean . . ."

Her voice trailed away. Not three hundred yards from where she stood, he was setting a post to mark the westernmost corner of their entire claim area. She could hear the rhythmic pounding of his sledgehammer driving it in. But when molten ore had flowed through the neighboring rock there hadn't been any reservation lines. How could he be so sure there wasn't more gold over here, under her very feet? The answer came before she had clearly formed the question. He didn't know, but he suspected. Hadn't his frantic search for the spout begun when the tests near the reservation proved so much better than he expected?

She sat down suddenly, struck with certainty. Not only was there gold, but she knew why, despite mounting evidence, this was one area he refused to search. Not because of the reservation lines, but because he had promised Henry Kingbird the power place would be safe. Somewhere nearby was the spot Matt had sworn to protect.

And now a rival prospector had staked a claim. But who? They would have heard about any strangers in the area. The Indian network passed news more effectively than a rural party line. One of the Indians themselves? Whoever he was, if the forest already had begun to cover his traces, the filing office had had plenty of time to register his claim.

Heartsick for Matt's sake, she pulled back the brush to examine the stump. A rusty nail stuck out of the weathered wood, but if claim papers had been attached to it, they'd disappeared. Could it have served some other purpose? she wondered. As marker for the power place itself, perhaps? But who'd need a marker if the place was supposed to send out light? A claim stake made more sense. She'd cleared enough brush to know claims were outlined from stake to stake. Her sense of direction might be lousy, but if there was another square-cut stump, the faint path leading through the underbrush should take her to it.

To describe the trail as cleared was an exaggeration. The farther she went, the more it seemed like nothing but a highway for oversized wildlife. Bear, maybe. Or moose. Obedient to Matt's warnings, she'd never strayed far alone. If she didn't see anything on the other side of that outcrop, she told herself, it would be time to yell for company. She scrambled over the rock, using her hands to pull herself up. And because she looked down to check how straight she'd climbed, the glint beneath her left foot caught her eye.

She almost fell from shock. Even allowing for the fact that she had gold on the brain, a shimmer like that meant only one thing. Surface ore. This could be the spout! With her heart hammering from more than her climb, she dropped back to where light caught the hint of color and began to tear at the moss and dirt. The gleam spread.

"Matt!" she screamed. *"Matt!"*

Even across the distance, alarm rang in his voice. "Don't move! I'm coming!"

"Hurry! I'm all right, but hurry!"

Before she caught sight of him, she heard crashing in the underbrush and ran toward the sound. His arms closed around her, squeezing her breathless for an instant. "Are you hurt? What happened?"

"I found gold!"

He released her with a stifled exclamation.

"I think it's the spout! Isn't that fantastic?" Half stumbling in her excitement, she dragged him toward the rock with one hand, gesturing with the other. "See? It is the spout, isn't it? I've made the classic accidental find!"

As he ran his fingers over the exposed rock the way a blind man might explore a surface strewn with broken glass, his pallor increased. "Gold all right."

"You're in shock, aren't you? So am I. I feel like

Humphrey Bogart. I feel like I homered in the miners' World Series. Oh, Matt." She buried her delight against the broad expanse of his chest. "I'm lucky for you after all, aren't I? Lamartine-Holiday. We might have missed it if I hadn't come this way."

"That's right. We might have missed it."

His dull tone and the unexpected tremor in the hand stroking her hair made her look up. "Is anything wrong?" she asked.

"No." His arms tightened and his attempt at laughter faltered. "I'm still stunned, I guess. Now I know how it would feel to lose you."

"Don't look so grim. You didn't lose me."

"Not yet."

She snuggled back into the circle of his arms. Being close to him again was her reward. "We'll have to file right away. I don't care about the rest, but I'd hate to see anyone beat me to my own find."

"Did you see the stump?" he asked slowly.

"That's why I started walking. My giant brain reviewed its fund of mining information and said, 'This path could be an old claim line, because why else would anyone square off a stump in the middle of nowhere?' But it's an Indian marker, isn't it?"

"You could call it that."

"For the power place?"

"In a way."

"Well," she sighed, "then it's all right. I admit that when I saw it I was plenty worried. But if I hadn't worried, we wouldn't be standing here, umpteen thousands richer. In fact, after we move your post we can afford to take the day off."

"One last afternoon?"

She lifted a radiant face. "Just for us."

Sweetened by her exhilaration, familiar sights and smells around the camp stood out with special clarity for Nita: the crunch of pine needles underfoot, the ash-blue oval bodies of geese patrolling the margin of the lake like old friends, dark clouds piling up in the

west to turn the sunset into an exotic, gilt-edged cele-
bration. Yet tomorrow they'd be leaving, and imminent
departure lent each gesture a poignancy that etched in
her mind. The glow after an icy bath. Dismantling the
fishing weir on the stream. The last sunset. Now the
last campfire.

Quieter than usual, Matt finished his chores long
before she'd packed away the cooking gear, and he
stretched out beside the dying fire, his eyes following
her movements in and out of the light. "Leave it," he
said at last. "Come sit with me."

She tucked herself against the curve of his body, one
arm resting on his side, fingers tracing lazy circles on
his back. "I can't believe we'll be gone tomorrow," she
said.

"Are you sorry?"

She met his eyes. If she reached out, she could touch
the locks of black hair, the planes of his face, the lobes
of his ears. But how to touch the source of that dark,
urgent look? Now was the moment he might confirm
his need for her. Begin afresh. Speak the words to keep
her by his side. The thought hung in the air between
them, yet time poured through the silence like sand
through an hourglass. So few hours left, she thought.
Could he let them pass without claiming her?

"I'm sorry to be leaving," she said, turning her head
away.

"Not about anything else?"

"Not . . . unless you've changed the way you feel about
me."

He threaded his fingers through hers and their palms
met. "You have more right to change than I."

"Geese mate forever," she murmured. "Have you
forgotten?"

"Unscientific."

"I thought it was romantic."

"Tomorrow we're headed back to reality."

The hollow between their hands beat with a double
pulse. It might have been her heart he held. "Are you
saying . . . we'll never come back here?"

"I want you with me."

"But only here?"

"Nita!"

"That sounds like what you're suggesting. Romantic interludes that won't get in the way of the rest of your life."

Using their hands as a lever, he dragged her down against his chest. "Don't even think that to yourself," he said roughly. "I might not deserve your trust, but you are the one thing I ever truly wanted. From the moment I saw you. And every time I tried to tell you who I was and bit it back, the reason was my fear of losing you. Doubt everything else, but don't doubt that."

"Then why can't you ask for me?"

"Do you think I don't want to ask? In the beginning, when I knew making love to you would turn my life upside down, I couldn't stop what was happening any more than I could brake an avalanche. But even then I never guessed what it would mean to have you with me every day and night. Or how I'd feel today when I heard you call."

Her breath grazed his cheek. "Don't theorize. Don't explain. Just ask me."

With a groan, he captured her lips. Lacing the fingers of his right hand through her hair, he held her with as much force as though she were struggling to escape instead of welcoming his mouth with a need as avid as his own.

"I love you," she breathed when she could speak.

"Things change."

"But all change isn't bad!"

He lifted their joined hands, silhouetting them against the flickering embers. "You see this? Right now our lives mesh the way your hand fits mine—like fingers interlaced so tightly you can't separate them with your eye—yet one pull could divide them. I can't conceive of wanting to let you go, but I've no right to hold you."

"Did I say I wanted to go?"

"We're two separate people."

"Free to stay together if we want," she said, tightening her hand fiercely. "As free to stay as to go."

"Nita . . ."

"I love you. We've been changing all summer, but nothing's changed the way I feel about you. I thought I wanted you in my life. Now I'm sure. And I'm willing to gamble on the future." Smiling, she kissed him again. "Besides, with my sense of direction, I wouldn't dare let you out of my sight."

"One more night together?"

"At least one more."

"We shouldn't waste it."

She shook her head, feeling his heart begin to pound with her own. "Not in arguments about whether I care enough."

"Those can wait until tomorrow."

"I'll feel the same."

"And with my luck," he said with a wry smile, "I'll probably want you more than ever."

Two people could not undress at the same time in the small space of the tent. Nita lit the lantern while Matt stripped with the economy of motion that gave his movements so much grace. The light burnished his bronzed back, hardened by weeks of work, and she couldn't resist reaching out to feel its bosses and hollows ripple beneath her fingertips.

"You're splendid, you know," she said softly. "Just you. The way you are."

"Any good there is belongs to you."

"I feel the same."

He groaned as he turned to undress her, lingering over each revelation as though time and pleasure could be drawn out by force of will. Belonging to him by fullness of desire before they touched, she lay back at last, naked against the luxurious fur, whose caress was matched in delicacy by Matt's hands and mouth.

Could she doubt he loved her? she asked herself. Not when he squandered all of passion's range as if one night were meant to be the sum of weeks of loving. He stopped her breath with kisses, proved against his own argument that limbs as well as lives could mesh and twine, lavished his ardor like seed to be sown, then reaped and sowed again. And when at last the sweet, shared cry of union left them spent and giddy in each other's arms, he had the strength to crush her to him still.

"Don't leave me, Nita!"

Stroking his back, she hovered between pleasure's release in laughter and anxiety's release in tears. "As if I could."

The next morning they loaded the canoe in an unfriendly drizzle. "Could be worse," Nita said, grinning although her teeth chattered against a final cup of tea. "The paddles could freeze in mid-stroke."

"We'd be stuck for the winter."

"Hey, that's your first smile of the day!"

He knotted down the tarp and accepted a share of her tea, watching her over the rim of the mug as he drank. "I'd rather stay than go."

"You're just worrying about making our find public. I'll bet you're picturing prospectors' tents pitched every ten feet all the away from here to the reservation by next summer."

He groaned. "If that were the only problem!"

"We can't look back, Matt. Be glad you'll have more control over Holiday Mines than if that stump meant someone else had filed claims on the site."

"At least then I'd be in the clear."

"Everyone trusts you."

"Worse luck!"

He looked so haggard as he ran one hand through his hair, she kissed the damp strands. "We'll work it out," she said, taking the mug from him. "I trust you too."

"Nita, don't say that!"

"But it's true.'

"Look, there's something I—"

"No," she interrupted, smiling. "Not one more pessimistic word. We're going to drop off the canoe, file the claims we've given our word to file, take the next plane to Houghton, do our best to make the mine a benefit instead of a blight, and live happily ever after. That's it, end of discussion, all anybody could expect of two mere humans. Now, do you want to take a last look around before we shove off? Say au-revoir-but-not-good-bye to the geese? Perform some other delaying, sentimental ritual?"

He smiled. "Is kissing you delaying?"

"Well, since you put it that way, what's the rush?"

Muffling her in his embrace, he rocked her back and forth as though he never intended to let her go. "Do you have any idea how much I love you?"

"Enough to take me back to central heating?"

He released her, laughing shakily. "If that's what you want."

By the time they reached town and stored the canoe, Nita had announced and asked Matt's opinion on enough plans to occupy all the years until their retirement and alter the prospects of Indians all over the province. They hiked to the post office for the last mail, said good-bye to Jimmy, stunned Matt's niece with Blake's photographs of her and the unexpected vision of a career in New York, and promised the blanket weaver $450 for every one she delivered. The Indian network had been busy. So many people came to see them off on their Bearskin flight, the pilot shook his head, surmising they must have been the biggest tippers in the history of fishing.

As they walked into the claims office building in Thunder Bay, Nita, at a fever pitch of excitement, began to fret at Matt's diffidence. Although she was disappointed to find their destination a modern courthouse on a street complete with a corner cabstand, instead of a plank shelter complete with saddle horses tied outside, she tugged at his arm as they climbed the stairs. "How can you be so blasé? I couldn't be more nervous if we were going to a justice of the peace."

"Nita, will you wait a—"

"Oh, stop stalling, Matt!" she cried, turning the knob of the glass-windowed door leading into the office. "We're about to make history and you act as if people discovered major gold lodes every summer!"

At the sound of a feminine voice, the claims agent

snapped his sandy-haired head up in surprise, but he recognized Matt. "How about that! You must be getting lucky at more than mining, Lamartine. Is this a social call?"

"Nope."

"Life and death, by the look of you. Well, it's been slow around here since the last time you were in. I could use a bit of excitement."

Glowing, Nita took the papers Matt failed to offer the agent and spread them out on the counter. "These will make your day."

"Think you've found something good, eh?"

The man's sharp Adam's apple protruded over his shirt collar as he stretched his head from photographs to section maps to assay results. Matt moved away, but Nita hung over the meridians and baselines as though land measurement packed all the emotional wallop of romance. "Pretty sensational stuff, huh?" she said.

"Not bad for cleaning up odds and ends."

"You call those odds and ends?" she exclaimed.

He smiled. "Only compared to what he filed before."

"Before?"

"Last fall about this time, wasn't it?"

She turned slowly toward Matt. Braced against the wall, his pack slung over one shoulder, he had his eyes fixed on her as though waiting for this moment. "What does he mean," she whispered, "about filing before?"

"My original claim was filed last year."

"Yup," the agent rambled on cheerfully, "by the looks of what you've got here, that one was a real doozer. The assays seemed pretty good at the time, of course, but if you've got a spout in an area like this, why, you'll blow the lid off the mining community for sure. Those boys from Toronto are going to be gnashing their teeth, and I'll have more prospectors in here next year than we've seen for the last forty."

But Nita barely heard what the man said. Her pulse thundered in her ears. So Matt had filed a valuable claim last fall. Long before they'd met. Before he'd thought of asking for her backing, met her family, or talked to her of trust without offering any of his own.

Struggling for air, she stared at the man who suddenly seemed a stranger. "Then you cut that stump?"

"Yes, but—"

"You knew about the gold all along."

"Nita, I swear to you when I filed I—"

"Swear?" she said bitterly. "What good would that do, Matt Lamartine? Who could trust one word you said?"

Ten

The claims agent looked from Matt's pale face to Nita's flushed one, his Adam's apple working up and down in embarrassment. "I guess I spoke out of turn?"

"You did me a favor," Nita said. "My partner thinks none of his past is worth mentioning. My ex-partner."

"Nita, let me explain."

"Four months ago I would have believed your explanations without question. After the powwow I gave you another chance. Any time during the last two weeks I still would have tried to understand. But it's too late for excuses now. Way too late!"

As she started toward the door Matt grabbed her arm and spun her around. "I won't let you go without hearing me out. I made that claim for one purpose—to create a buffer zone that would keep any aboveground mining at a distance from the reservation line. I don't consider it my land. I never thought of mining there. You have to believe that."

"Why should I?"

Shaking off his hand, she left both the door and the claims agent's mouth standing wide open and headed toward the front entrance. Matt followed one step behind her.

"Will you listen for just a minute? Beyond getting the assays to prove the claim last year, I hadn't even checked it out. The fact that you practically fell over the spout ought to make that obvious! In order to revalidate my claim, all I had to do was bring in a minimal amount of ore every year. I calculated the neighboring lode was rich enough so I could pick up what I needed along the margins."

In the entranceway she turned to him. "Congratulations. Sounds as though you're a better con man than an engineer."

"Nita, ending up with the most easily minable section of the lode was the furthest thing from my mind. Accuse me of moronic carelessness, if you want. Lord knows, I deserve it. But I had no intention of cheating you or your family. What else can I say? I made a misjudgment and I've spent the last month searching my brains for some way to correct my mistake."

"You made more than one."

"I should have told you? Is that what you mean?"

"You should have told me a lot of things."

The hand he'd stretched out to her dropped to his side. When he leaned his head back against the wall with his eyes closed, he looked so drained she had to force herself not to weaken. No matter how valid his reasons for doing what he'd done, hadn't he traded on her feelings long enough? Hadn't Libby been right to say a woman had no future with a man who couldn't be completely frank?

"Well?" she asked mercilessly. "What kept you from telling me?"

Opening his eyes, he looked at her steadily. "The promise I'd made to Henry Kingbird and the tribal council to protect the power spot. The fact that the whole lode has turned out to be far richer than I expected and potentially so much more dangerous. Promises I made to myself when I began to realize what I'd started. One of the main reasons I couldn't tell you was that your aunt suspected me of doing exactly what you think I've done."

"But you didn't trust me to understand?"

"I didn't think in those terms."

"Maybe you should have," she said grimly.

"The problem was mine, not yours."

"So you shut me out. The way you shut me out right from the beginning."

"I'd given my word."

"Fine." Without looking at him she started marching toward the cabstand, seeing neither the street nor the passersby. "I can respect that. I wouldn't have asked you to sacrifice your promise. But together we could have come up with an answer. A neutral zone. A moratorium. Something. Your honor didn't have to be so one-sided that it excluded my family. Or me."

"I'm not excluding you. I want you to marry me."

With her hand on the door handle of the lone cab waiting at the stand, she looked back at him. "What kind of offer is that? Amends? A consolation prize for being such a good sport all these months?"

"Take everything I have, Nita. Do you think I give a damn about my share of the mine, except for your sake?"

"What you *have* is not the point!"

"I won't let you go like this."

Although his arm barred her way, she tugged at the door. Some passing businessmen glanced in their direction. Two women paused uncertainly for a moment, then scurried on. The driver's head rose up over the top of his cab. "Hey! Leave the lady alone. You want me to call a cop?"

"I'm not molesting her," Matt said through gritted teeth. "I'm asking her to marry me."

"That okay with you, lady?"

"No, it's not!" Prying at Matt's grip without success, she added hotly, "In the beginning, when you said you couldn't have a partner you didn't trust, money was supposed to be all I cared about. Well, you're a lot richer now than the day we met, and instead of begging you to stay, I'm leaving. That's how much I care about the money!"

The cabbie shook his head. "Looks like you got your answer, buddy."

"Can't we go somewhere and talk?" Matt pleaded.

She abandoned her struggle and faced him. "You had plenty of chances to talk. I was aching to listen. Maybe you never understood me, but you were right about one thing—a relationship can't exist without trust. And we still don't have it."

"Is that your final answer?"

"The principle's as valid now as it was before."

"Nita, please."

"It won't work, Matt. Your offer isn't good enough. The one change that counted, you didn't choose to make." When the words were out, she suddenly felt more tired than she'd ever been in her whole life. Every part of her body ached.

"You're all I ever wanted."

"Too bad," she said, pushing back her hair with a weary gesture. "You got yourself a mine instead. Talk to Russell about winding up the contract. He'll know how to handle the details."

"We have more than a contract, Nita."

"Not anymore."

His eyes held hers for a long moment, then slowly he stood aside to let her enter the cab.

The driver checked for nonexistent traffic as he pulled away from the curb. "Okay, lady, now you got that business settled, where to?"

"Airport, please," she said, leaning her head back and closing her eyes against the swell of tears.

Coming from Thunder Bay, the jangle and commotion at O'Hare shocked her. She'd forgotten about crowds waiting to meet arriving passengers, even larger crowds waiting to depart, the constant babble of voices and intercom announcements reverberating along the bustling corridors.

"Got a lot of stuff with you?" Russell shouted to her over the din. "I tipped a couple of redcaps to wait for us."

"No luggage."

"You're kidding!"

"Did you think I'd save the sleeping bag?"

He grinned. "Knew you'd appreciate that one."

She had, but continued mental health wouldn't tolerate reminders of how much. As they swept past the concession area on their way to the parking lot, she stopped in front of the bookstall. "Wait a sec, Russell."

"I already bought a paper." He flourished the one he carried folded under his arm. "Gold index is creeping up there. The twins' forecast was right on the button again."

"Do me a favor, Russell. Don't talk to me about gold."

Ignoring his puzzled look, she headed for the fiction section and systematically loaded one copy of every romance in stock into her arms. The selection wasn't too good, but it would keep her going over the weekend.

After she paid for them, Russell picked up the bundle of books with frowning concentration. "Is Lamartine staying north to clean up the paperwork?"

"To clean up, pure and simple. And do me another favor, will you? Don't mention Matthew Lamartine."

"Had a falling out huh?"

"Russell, what did I just say to you?"

"Win one, lose one," he said philosophically.

His nonchalant acceptance made Matt's disappearance from her life painfully real. Once her family recovered from their collective outrage at being cheated out of the most lucrative section of the claim, the name Lamartine would cease to be mentioned and Nita's escape judged a close call. Moving in their different worlds, she and Matt might never meet again. The prospect seemed so wretched she had difficulty keeping her voice steady. "How've you been, Russell?"

"Not bad. Since we broke ground on the new hotel, Gloria's been making noises about getting together again—sending singing telegrams to the office and that kind of stuff. But you know? I think I've outgrown her. Actually, I met this great woman playing racquetball at the club. Turns out she has twin brothers in San Jose. Struck me as a perfect chance to set up Cookie and Sugar, so I asked her to dinner."

"Motivated by sheer altruism."

He considered. "Well, I can't deny she's a good-looking woman. But I figure it's about time for me to start taking my family responsibilities seriously. Uncle Bo and Aunt Addy are getting on. Household full of unmarried sisters. Makes a fellow think."

"So if neither of the twins nibble, I'll inherit two chances?"

"Hey, that's right!" He looked at her with some admiration. "I hadn't worked it out that far ahead because I thought maybe you and Lamartine—"

"Russell!"

"Sorry." He held the car door open for her. "So do you have plans, or what?"

"Not yet."

"Take it from me, it's no good to sit around and brood," he assured her, nosing his Mercedes into the honking mass of vehicles leaving the airport. "Coming along when Gloria and I split up, Lamartine's gold deal—sorry—was a lifesaver. Tell you what, after you get your hair done and pull yourself together a little, we might work out a deal."

Her thoughts flew to the contract with Matt. Maybe the legalities of Lamartine-Holiday would bind them to communication after all. "Who's 'we'?"

"You and me. Who else?"

"Oh."

Paying no attention to her disappointment, Russell continued blithely. "I've been checking out the Trans-Canada Highway around the claim area. Do you realize the place is virtually without motels? What I have in mind is something with a lot of original decorator touches. You know, moose heads in the dining room, birchbark wastebaskets. That's where you come in."

She stared at him. "With the moose heads?"

"I figure we could stage some Indian ceremonies once a week. Put in a pen of deer for kids to pet. Canoe trips with costumed guides. Mine tours. A couple of boutiques specializing in gold jewelry. Everything for a real family vacation."

The thought of Matt's reaction if she arrived with a crew bent on actualizing Russell's version of Indian life made her shudder. "You want to build a Holidayland around the mine?"

"Holidayland! I like it!"

"Count me out, Russell."

Her vehemence startled him. "How come? Bound to be a big money-maker. We'll be sitting on spare land and there's nothing like it for miles."

"You'll change that place over my dead body."

"Hey, what's eating you all of a sudden? We're talking heap big bucks." He shot her a sidelong glance. "A project like this could throw you and Lamartine together again too."

In spite of her best efforts, tears filled Nita's eyes. "Will you shut up, Russell! There's so much you don't understand."

He nursed an aggrieved silence during the remainder of the trip. Not until they entered the apartment did he mutter, "All I can say is, four months in the woods did nothing for your disposition."

Aunt Addy looked up from pouring her nightcap. As though her niece had stepped around the corner on an errand only moments earlier, she asked vaguely, "Have a nice time, dear?"

Nita manufactured a wan smile.

"She left Lamartine up there," Russell said.

"Left him? Was that really wise, dear?"

"Oh, Aunt Addy, don't you start in too!"

Stifling a wail of misery, Nita fled to her room.

Each day that followed dulled her hope that Matt might come after her, and she fought to restore her equilibrium the way she had disciplined herself to take off extra inches with exercise as a Harrison model. Logic over sentiment, she told herself. Romance relegated to the printed page. But her heart wasn't in the new regime.

The twins arrived to spend the long Columbus Day weekend, overflowing with accounts of high-tech conquests in Silicon Valley and forays into San Francisco. When the strain of their enthusiasm and Russell's allusions to love's golden hours grew too great, Nita hiked for hours along the lake. Although she tried to push thoughts of the summer from her mind, the sight of children playing ball, giant Canadas pausing on their southward flight, or a sudden memory of the look on Matt's face when she left him always drove her home missing him more than ever.

Brooding in Chicago was accomplishing nothing. She made a plane reservation to New York for the following Monday and hauled out her luggage. As she began to excavate her drawers and closets, she wondered when she had intended to wear such clothes. Over-the-elbow Chantilly lace gloves? A beaver coat dyed in stripes of purple, gold, and rose? Pumps and a matching hand-bag of tinted python skin? She weeded swiftly and ruthlessly. Her excisions pleased her until she stepped back to view the result and discovered a wardrobe precisely tailored for wintering in a certain university town in northern Michigan.

When Uncle Bo peered around her door, she was sitting amid the strewn garments, hugging herself as though she could contain the ache inside. He held out a bulky parcel.

"Package for you, Ni."

With a cry of joy she leaped up to scan the hand-lettered wrapper. A Michigan postmark. Color spread over her face with the lurch of her heart. Dumping the package on the bed, she tore into the brown paper. Fur billowed out like a captured cloud, but she pushed it aside to scrabble through the wrappings for any scrap of writing. Nothing. She shook the blanket feverishly. A pair of new moccasins and a mouth-bow lay inside.

Holding them in her hands, she sank onto the bed and stared out the window. Her mind's eye was fixed not on Chicago's stone, steel, and glass, but on the marshy fringe of a long, narrow lake, where a family of long-necked geese paddled in stately progression past a small domed tent surrounded by birches whose sunlit yellow leaves glowed brighter than gold.

"No letter?" Uncle Bo asked.

"No."

"Maybe not in so many words, but I'd say the gist's plain enough. You still moping after him, Ni?"

"I can't help myself."

"Got to take people the way they come, you know." Her uncle shook his head. "Why, water always made Ad squeamish unless it was in a tub, and I never did get the hang of riding a horse. She thought I should have hustled more; I used to tell her she had greater sympathy for a stallion than a human being. But she's a smart woman. I did right not to let her go."

At the far end of the hall slamming doors, raised voices, and rustling papers announced the twins' return from a shopping spree at Field's. "We'd better ask Nita before we do it," Sugar was saying.

"Russell says she hasn't heard from him for weeks."

"But *we* never heard from him at *all*."

"Maybe he's changed his—"

The hall telephone cut short Cookie's rebuttal. Squealing, both twins rushed to answer it, but Nita scarcely heard the extension ringing beside her bed.

"Matt wasn't open with me, Uncle Bo," she said. "He'd talk about any subject in the world, yet all the time his mind was running in secret compartments he wouldn't share. Not even," she added bitterly, "when I was concerned."

"I suppose you told him all about those other fellows of yours? Just to give him the idea?"

"They had nothing to do with how I feel about him!"

"Better listen to yourself, Ni. Maybe you two aren't as far apart as you think. A man's only human. And a woman, too, of course. Doing the best they can for each other, but managing a fair number of mistakes between 'em. Ought to give the fellow credit if he's learning as he goes."

"You think I'm being too hard on Matt?"

"Depends on how much you're hoping he'll come up to scratch." Her uncle patted her arm. "Ad's been trying to get me from a trot to a canter for over forty years."

He ambled toward the door as the twins' heads appeared around it. "Phone's for you, Nita," Cookie said.

"It's long distance."

Matt. The blood drained from Nita's head so suddenly she grew dizzy. Who else might call her long distance? Fighting for calm, she snatched the receiver in both hands. Bottled feelings choked her voice.

Libby's greeting flowed over the phone line like warm molasses, but Nita flopped back onto her pillows, too drained by disappointment to respond in kind. "I thought you might be Matt," she said.

The twins, who had pounced on the abandoned blanket with cries of delight, stopped admiring the fur long enough to exchange significant looks at the mention of Matt's name. Leaving the room at such an interesting juncture would never occur to either of them.

"He called," Libby said.

Nita swallowed. "Matt called you?"

"Actually, he wanted Blake. Something about sending his niece's pictures to Harrison."

"Oh."

"I asked about you."

Nita's palms prickled with moisture. Her mouth felt dry. "What did he say?"

"He sounded even bleaker than you."

"Serves him right."

Cookie began rummaging through Nita's discards to justify lingering. She held up a puffed and pleated gown of metallic tissue for elaborate consideration. Kneeling on the end of the bed, Sugar was examining the construction of the blanket as exhaustively as an apprentice tanner.

"Couldn't you forgive him?" Libby said.

Nita groaned. "How many times?"

"As many as you can."

"Oh, come off it, Lib. You're the one who said it would never work unless I could trust him."

"I know." Libby sighed. "That's why I had to call. Blake and I talked about you two for a long time. He thinks I gave you a bum steer—laying down arbitrary standards as though people's experiences were the same. He says Matt probably has had to use his independence as a defense all his life. With everything at stake in this case, it wouldn't be fair to expect him to open up overnight."

"Four months isn't overnight."

"Compared to thirty years?"

"But he had no reason to treat me like the enemy. I was killing myself to prove I was on his side."

"Be reasonable, Nita."

"Who can be reasonable? I lost my common sense that day in Rare Books!"

"Well, now you need it back. I know you can't handle feelings with logic, but you have to try. By nature you're the most totally frank person I ever knew. But Blake's right. Not everybody's the same."

"I've heard that before. I've even *said* it."

"Making a commitment was easier for you than for Matt," Libby persisted. "You weren't being pulled in two directions. He was. He'd taken on a lot of responsibilities before he met you. You wouldn't have wanted him to throw those over without a thought. Give him credit for trying to come to terms with them with as much integrity as he has. You said he never lied to you. Can't you believe his explanation now? Didn't he face the Holidays en masse for your sake? Didn't he want you to be part of everything except his past?"

Nita digested this assessment in silence. "So what's your advice?"

"The same as you gave me. If you still care, go after him."

"That's what you think, huh?"

"That's what I *know*."

"I should change my flight for one to Houghton?"

"Face it, friend, he's the first man to keep you interested for four weeks, let alone four months. Just because he isn't perfect doesn't mean he isn't right."

"He sent me a new pair of moccasins."

"For a fresh start." Libby's chuckle warmed the line. "Call me from Houghton."

Nita hung up the phone and lay still so long that the twins lost patience. Tossing aside the dress, Cookie said, "We were wondering how you'd feel—"

"If we invited Matt down to Monterey," Sugar finished in a rush.

Nita raised herself on one elbow. Their eager faces

brought a sympathetic smile to her mouth. "Take the dress, Cookie. It'll look terrific on you. The blanket has sentimental value, but you can have that too. For luck. In fact, take anything you fancy. Anything," she added firmly, "except Matt."

"But Russell said you—"

"And Matt were finished."

"Since when," Nita said with asperity, "has our brother Russell become an authority on women?"

She hummed as she brushed her hair the next morning. Outside her window a boundless, untroubled blue backed the Chicago skyline. Sunshine flowed into the room, making motes of dust glitter in the light. Another golden day. Perfect for camping on someone's doorstep.

Filled with benevolence toward the world, she headed for her last breakfast as one of Russell's burdensome unmarried sisters. His voice stopped her in the hall.

"So help me," he was saying over the breakfast clink of china and glass, "when I read his proposal, my first thought was that the man had had a breakdown. Gone clean off his rocker."

"Poor Matt!" Cookie sighed. Then her voice brightened. "But he must need someone—"

"To look after him!" Sugar exclaimed.

"No need to dramatize, dears," Aunt Addy said. "I'm sure your brother spoke metaphorically. I suppose the proposal involved the mine?"

Nita's pulses quickened. Had Matt chosen today to report on his claim? How would her family react when she announced that she understood why he'd done what he'd done and refused to give him up? Whatever their response, it would be explosive enough to earn this breakfast a lasting place in the Holiday family annals.

"Morning, everyone," she said. "Talking business?"

Stuffing a wad of toast into his mouth, Russell shot his wrist out of his cuff to check his watch as though he were timing her entrance. "Hey, we're allowed to mention the mine again! You must be in better mood this morning."

"I am."

"Your brother has received a most disturbing message, dear."

"Mmm?"

"I'll show the stuff to the legal department tomorrow, Aunt Addy," Russell continued, "but it reads okay. The basic idea is what's so screwy. He's offering us his entire share in the lode if we agree to prevent any aboveground excavation, construction, or transportation within a ten-mile radius of the point he specifies."

Nita stared at her brother. The power place! That had to be the point Matt picked. Did this offer to her family mean he'd found some way to protect it after all? But how? When she'd walked into the room she'd been prepared to defend his reason for filing the early claim. Now she hardly knew what to think.

"The boy has some trick up his sleeve," Uncle Bo growled. "He's not the type to throw his game."

Aunt Addy's voice sharpened. "Your uncle is right, Russell. There are some legal shenanigans involved here. I seem to remember that claiming the surface land automatically conveys the right to follow any vein found within those lines?"

"Give me some credit. That's the first thing I checked. In Canada, surface rights go straight down, just the *opposite* of what you said. You could be onto a vein as wide as the Mississippi and where your claim ended and another guy's claim began, all you'd be able to do would be to watch him shovel it up. But that's the nutty thing about the way Lamartine frames his offer. *We'd* keep anything underground."

Nita caught her breath in a sudden rush of comprehension. Matt wasn't simply protecting the power place. He was baiting his proposal in a way that proved the gold he'd found meant nothing to him.

"His sole condition is that we not develop this one area?" Aunt Addy sounded genuinely baffled.

"That's it."

"What do we know about this area?"

"Beats me why he picked it. On the survey map it's about five hundred yards inside the reservation boundaries and there's nothing there but trees. Would a man in his right mind trade his share of a strike like the one Lamartine brought in for a clump of firewood that belongs to the Indians anyway?"

"But, Russell," Cookie exclaimed, "we just put out a buy signal on gold. Matt's percentage of the lode—"

"Could be worth a fortune!" Sugar finished with a gasp.

Uncle Bo frowned. "Hate to say it, Ad, but Russell may have a point. Poor fellow's gone off the deep end."

Aunt Addy viewed her husband with irritation. "Don't be absurd. For some reason this spot he's chosen is more valuable than he lets on. Nita, dear, surely you have some idea what he has in mind?"

The combined Holiday stare turned in Nita's direction, and she tried to collect her thoughts. Her family might think Matt crazy, but his proposal was so bold it dazzled her. In one gesture, he'd canceled his obligation to her family, found a way to protect the power spot, and sent her a message that she was the only thing he wanted. A romance hero couldn't have done it better. Now it was up to her to help him get rid of the fortune she had helped him find. She raised her eyes to her family's expectant faces and said simply, "This is the first I've heard about Matt's plan."

The twins looked at each other.

Uncle Bo shook his head. "Steadiest hand on the cue I ever saw. Never would have believed his mind would go."

"Nonsense," Aunt Addy snapped. "Get him down here, Russell."

"I'm way ahead of you, Aunt Addy. I sent him a wire this morning that should bring him on the double." Frantic peals of the doorbell almost drowned out Russell's words. While the maid hurried to the door, he checked his watch again. "In fact it sounds like he made pretty good time."

"Where is she?"

Nita's mouth dropped at the sound of Matt's voice.

Russell grinned across the table at her. "I wired him you'd had an accident. 'Your name her last conscious word' and all that."

"You didn't!"

"Would I kid you? There's real money at stake here."

To her brother's evident astonishment, Nita flung her arms around his neck and kissed him soundly before she flew down the hall into Matt's arms.

He crushed her against his chest. "Are you all right?"

"For the first time in weeks."

"I nearly went crazy when I got your brother's wire. I hired a plane to get here. I don't even know what I thought. I was afraid you were dying."

"Isn't a private plane an extravagance for a professor who's giving away his fortune?" she asked, luxuriating in the feeling of arms bound around her in a grip that would have done a drowning man proud.

"You heard about my offer?"

"My family thinks you're dotty," she said, laughing.

"You know why I had to do it?"

She raised her hand to smooth away the ravages of anxiety that still shadowed his features. "I know."

"I'm back to square one, Nita. I don't owe anyone anything, but I've nothing to offer you."

"Nothing?"

He groaned and pressed her closer. "Only what I feel."

"Not such a bad offer."

"Before your cab left the curb, I knew I had to get you back. My head's been so full of schemes to deal with the situation, everyone in Houghton probably thinks I'm crazier than your family does."

"You came up with a great plan."

"Nothing to it," he said, smiling at her. "By the time I'd replayed every moment we had spent together for the hundredth time, what you said in Thunder Bay finally hit me."

"What did I say?"

"About creating a neutral zone."

"Hey, that makes the idea a team effort. You know, if we started pulling in the same direction, we might change the world."

"I think we're on the right track."

"If that's a proposal, I accept."

"Could you live on a professor's salary?"

"What do you mean?" she said indignantly. "I'm going to make a killing in the blanket business!"

He laughed, and as he bent toward her she lifted her lips to his. All the feelings she'd stored up to tell him, she offered in her kiss: acceptance, trust strengthened by forgiveness, the infinite joy of communion. And the sweetness of his mouth on hers answered with an equal depth of love.

"No more secrets?" she asked when their lips parted.

"Can't think of anything I haven't told you," he murmured, "except that I don't eat brussels sprouts."

"Minor."

"Or caviar."

"Libby might mind, but I don't."

He smiled. "There was one other significant woman in my life."

"Besides your mother?"

"Yup. My fourth-grade teacher. I was desperately in love with her until we hit fractions."

"Understandable."

As she relaxed deeper into his arms, he said, "Actually, there is one other thing. I checked out a house for us. Right on the shore."

"With a big porch facing the lake and a stone fireplace?"

"Mmm."

"Fantastic!"

"But I didn't rent it."

"Why not?"

He kissed her again. "I didn't want to risk making any more decisions behind your back. Indian men are insecure, you know. That's what makes them so possessive and hard for women to handle."

"Insecure!" she scoffed. "You? The man who has my family holding its collective breath in the other room?"

"They haven't bought my offer yet?"

"You think we might not live happily after all?" she cried in mock horror.

"I wouldn't go that far."

"Whew!"

"Still, the safest plan would be to tackle them to-gether."

Wriggling out of his arms, she smiled up at him. "Now you're talking, partner." With his hands clasping hers, they headed for the dining room. "Lamartine-Holiday can handle *anything*."

THE EDITOR'S CORNER

Last month I briefly told you the good news that The Delaney Dynasty lives on! Next month you'll get a sneak preview of the second trio of Delaney books, **THE DELANEYS OF KILLAROO,** in a Free Sampler you'll see everywhere! It's part of a promotion that is unique in publishing history and is being done jointly by LOVESWEPT and Clairol®. In the late fall last year, a creative and effervescent young woman representing Clairol, Inc., came to see us at Bantam. Their market research had identified the "perfect user" of a new hair product they were developing as the same woman who reads LOVESWEPT romances! You, my friends out there, were described as intelligent, clever, fun loving, optimistic, romantic women who cared about and tried to make a contribution to family, friends, community, and country. Sounds right to me, I said. The new product from Clairol®—PAZAZZ® SHEER COLORWASH—is a continuation of the PAZAZZ® line of temporary (and, I must add, fun) coloring gels, mousses, and color wands. But what truly amazed me was that one of the colors they had "invented"—*Sheer Plum*—had just been "invented" by Fayrene Preston for her heroine Sydney in **THE DELANEYS OF KILLAROO.** Further, while Iris Johansen's and Kay Hooper's heroines weren't described in the precise terms of the new Clairol® colors, they were so close that one had to begin to believe that our two companies were fated to get together with **THE DELANEYS OF KILLAROO** and **PAZAZZ® SHEER COLORWASH**. So we decided to do a promotion featuring a Sampler of the new books about the Australian branch of the Delaney family, whose heroines had Sheer Colorwash hair colors. And in each Sampler Clairol® gives you a Beauty Bonus full of tips on hair beauty and styling using the new products. Next month at health and beauty aid sections of stores and at cosmetic counters you will find the Free Sampler. You'll also find the Free Samplers when you go to your local bookselling outlet. In all, more than three-quarters of a million copies of these Samplers will be given away during a six-week period. Then, when **THE DELANEYS OF KILLAROO** books are published in August, the first 200,000 copies of each title will carry a special money-saving coupon from Clairol® so that you—you "perfect users" you!—can try
(continued)

PAZAZZ® SHEER COLORWASH at a lower price. I hope you'll enjoy this promotion since you are its special focus. Lots of other women who may never have heard of LOVE-SWEPT romances will learn about them, too, as all of us learn for the first time about a brand-new way to put more PAZAZZ® into our lives with color highlights ranging from subtle to dramatic ... from the glints of gold in Sheer Cinnamon or Amber to the glow of a fine wine in Sheer Plum or Burgundy. We on the LOVESWEPT staff have been treated by Clairol® to samples of all these products ... and if you could see us now! We, in turn, treated the Clairol® ladies to the Delaney books and other LOVESWEPTs, and they loved them! We've had so much fun with this promotion, and we hope you, too, will enjoy this first-ever promotion with you in mind.

Now for a few words about the delightful LOVESWEPTs in store for you next month.

We are so pleased to introduce a wonderful new talent, Glenna McReynolds, making her debut as a published author with **SCOUT'S HONOR,** LOVESWEPT #198. In this charming love story Mitch Summers, a wonderfully masterful and yet vulnerable man, follows stunningly beautiful Anna Lange from San Francisco to the Bahamas to ask her a simple favor: would she turn her gambling skills on a cheating cardsharp and win back the land his brother lost in a crooked poker game? After a disastrous experience with a fortune hunter, Anna holds all men at arm's length, but she cannot resist Mitch's boyish charm ... or his passionate kisses. With the glamour of high stakes poker and with the heart-warming emotion of sensuous romance, this is a fabulous first love story from Glenna McReynolds.

Prepare to be glued to your chair, unable to put down **ALLURE,** LOVESWEPT #199, by Fayrene Preston. Breath-takingly passionate and emotional, **ALLURE** is the love story of Rick O'Neill and Chandra Stuart, star-crossed lovers who meet once more after years apart. Only Rick can't remember very much about Chandra, and she has never been able to forget a single thing about him! Then, haunted by a scent that brings along with it a powerful memory, Rick begins to unravel the mystery of the past ... and blaze a trail toward a future with the woman he loves. An enthralling, powerful romance.

(continued)

We are delighted to announce that Joan Bramsch—author of such wonderful, beloved LOVESWEPTs as **THE SOPHISTI- CATED MOUNTAIN GAL** and **THE STALLION MAN**—has the distinction of being the author of our two-hundredth LOVESWEPT, **WITH NO RESERVATIONS**! Hotel executive Ann Waverly is understandably intrigued by Jeffrey Madison. The first time she meets him he looks like something the cat dragged in; the second time, he's wearing only a sheet! Jeffrey is powerfully attracted to Ann, but his suspicious actions make her wary of him and the potent effect he has on her senses. Actually, both Ann and Jeffrey have their secrets, and you'll be kept on the edge of your seat as Joan skillfully weaves this tale of humor and deep love.

Linda Cajio gives us another lighthearted and touching romance with **RESCUING DIANA,** LOVESWEPT #201. At a reception Adam Roberts is captivated by Diana Windsor— nicknamed Princess Di—an endearingly innocent and shy creator of computer games. Diana is equally enchanted by Adam—he's her knight in shining armor come to life. But neither Adam nor Diana expected he would *really* have to rescue this princess from all sorts of modern-day dragons. As you follow Adam and Diana from one delightful escapade to another, you'll fall as much in love with them as they do with each other.

Enjoy!
Warm regards,

Carolyn Nichols

Carolyn Nichols
   Editor
LOVESWEPT
Bantam Books, Inc.
666 Fifth Avenue
New York, NY 10103

NEW!

Handsome Book Covers Specially Designed To Fit Loveswept Books

Our new French Calf Vinyl book covers come in a set of three great colors—royal blue, scarlet red and kachina green.

Each 7" × 9½" book cover has two deep vertical pockets, a handy sewn-in bookmark, and is soil and scratch resistant.

To order your set, use the form below.